Hey, I'm Iffat! I wrote this book. Now, before you read this, let me give my fellow readers a simple note:

THIS WAS NOT INSPIRED BY *AVATAR*.

The *AVATAR* show; Aang, Sokka, Katara, the lot. This surprisingly was never inspired by that series! (But I do love it greatly.) I was surprised when I watched the show and thought, *Woah. My book is so similar!* But I will not lie about the fact that some names have been inspired by the epic lego universe *Bionicle*. You'll see how soon! I feel my book revolves around many themes and has been influenced by many stories – too many to count. So, enjoy reading because there is certainly more to keep coming from this franchise and maybe even more separate stories to come for all to enjoy.

Iffat Bhuiyan was born in Rome and moved to London. He is a creative and ambitious teenager who studies in secondary school. His interests include drawing, writing, history and culture. When he's not writing, he tends to draw, play games (mostly flight simulators and historical shooters) or scour the internet for Italian courses (he has forgotten it all). He lives with his parents, his twin brother and his elder sister. And whilst he has no pet, he either dreams of having a cat, a hawk, or a Royal Bengal tiger (because why not).

I dedicate this book to my family and all those who have supported me. Your help is what helped this book become what it is today.

Iffat Bhuiyan

LEGEND OF EKARTO:
THE STONES ARISE

AUSTIN MACAULEY PUBLISHERS™
LONDON • CAMBRIDGE • NEW YORK • SHARJAH

A CIP catalogue record for this title is available from the British Library.

ISBN 9781398459007 (Paperback)
ISBN 9781398459021 (ePub e-book)
ISBN 9781398459014 (Audiobook)

www.austinmacauley.com

First Published 2022
Austin Macauley Publishers Ltd®
1 Canada Square
Canary Wharf
London
E14 5AA

20230310

Thanks to the publishers for helping me realise a dream I thought would never come true, my family for reaching out to publishers to publish this book, my friends who read extracts and gave me more ideas to work with, and all the people in the team who designed, edited, marketed, and evolved this book from a Word document into an actual book.

Prologue

He lied in the crib, unharmed, crying and kicking his feet.

Ekarto was just born, two months earlier than he was supposed to. His mother was lying in a bed made from some twigs, logs and an even layer of fabrics, silk and cotton. She was unconscious. Alive but under a spell. Surrounding her was Ekarto's uncle, Okoto; his late dad's friend, Leaftor and some clerics from the castle. Ekarto's dad was dead. Killed by a bear in a cave, everyone said.

Okoto stared at the new-born. His innocent eyes gleaming in the moonlight. His eyes were quite pale – he was born blind. That ran in the family. Everyone was born blind until a couple of days had passed. It was nothing to worry about. That's what the clerics said.

Leaftor also stared at the new-born. He was ecstatic that his late friend's son was just born. He was covered in blood after the birth, but all Leaftor could see was Ekarto's dad. It was an unusual feeling to look at a baby and see a grown man's reflection off his face, but Ekarto seemed to be the closest thing to his dad Leaftor had now.

The clerics were wiping the blood off Ekarto's body ever so gently as not to hurt the baby. Ekarto was breathing deeply, even though it hurt every time he breathed. His mother was gaining consciousness slowly, and Ekarto didn't know it, but he wanted to be with his mother more than ever. The clerics helped his mother up and sat her up slightly with some extra cushions. She looked at her son for the first time, filled with joy. She couldn't hold back from holding him, even if her arms ached with every move.

"I'm here, Ekarto. I'm always here." She slowly rubbed Ekarto's back to let him go to sleep. But he wasn't going to sleep for long.

Okoto was walking to his guards and was talking to them. He kept looking to the baby and back at the guard he was talking to. It looked suspicious to Leaftor, but he decided to leave it and look back at the baby. He still couldn't believe his friend's son was born. It truly was unbelievable.

Ekarto started to feel sleepy. His eyelids became heavy, and his breathing reduced to slow, calm breaths. His mother was tired but happy. She was holding her son in her arms. Out of nowhere, two guards came to Ekarto's mother. They looked stern yet aloof.

"Lady Okinara, we must take the baby to the palace. He will be showered there, be greeted by the ministers and then be able to sleep with you."

"It's fine, guard. I want him to stay with me for a bit longer."

"Lady Okinara, it is an order from Emperor Okoto."

"Tell him I want Ekarto to stay with me. Dismissed, guard."

The guard scowled at Okinara and grabbed for the child. Okinara was startled, and Leaftor threw the guard to the other side. The other guard tried his best to grab Ekarto, but Leaftor shot a vine from the ground and up through the guard's stomach. He was born with the power of controlling vines and leaves. Three other guards dashed towards Leaftor and charged with halberds. Leaftor used the nearby trees' leaves to throw the guards back to the gates of the palace. The remaining guards charged at Leaftor, but he simply killed them all with more vines. Then he knew what to do.

"Okinara, I have to take Ekarto. He cannot stay here, it's too dangerous for him."

"No, Leaftor! He will stay with me!" Leaftor grunted and reluctantly snatched Ekarto from Okinara. Ekarto was startled and started to cry for his mother. Two guards chased Leaftor down the grounds, and three guards restrained Okinara. She screamed from the top of her lungs for her son. But Ekarto was too far away.

Leaftor slowed down as he walked down a secret path down the mountain nearby. He made sure to keep Ekarto safe. Ekarto was sleeping from exhaustion of screaming and crying. He could hear the footsteps of the guards, so he grew huge vines from the ground and created a rigid wall of vines and leaves. No one could go through the wall except if they were born with the same powers Leaftor had, and no one around had the powers.

Leaftor walked tirelessly until he found a boat floating on a lake. It was a small dingy, tied securely to a pole. Leaftor slashed the rope with a vine and sat in the boat. He used his powers to make the seaweed under him push the boat.

He knew exactly where he was going to send Ekarto.

The Mountain

"Right, you ready?"

Ekarto looked up at Mt Korkatar. It was the famed mountain that would apparently hold the mysterious and legendary Eldonville Kingdom. The mountain that Ekarto dreamed of climbing. After hours of riding horses through the endless plains that separated his village from the mountain, and another ride through the scorching deserts between the plains and a river that led to the mountain, he was finally here. Though the journey was exhausting, Ekarto was far too excited to even care about his tiredness. However, the mountain looked miniscule compared to when he saw it from his village. He imagined it to be a towering mountain capped with snow. But it was really just a big hill with grass on top. Nothing more. It did disappoint Ekarto, but he was also thankful he didn't have to climb so much.

The Silk villagers hated Eldonville for whatever reason that Ekarto wasn't allowed to know. However, his people's hatred for Eldonville did not stop his love for this great civilisation. Of its monarchs, its people, its wars and legends, its religions, so much all in just one kingdom. He was delighted when the priests in Silk Village told him he could go there, but he had to return before the sun sets – or else spirits would roam around and cause pandemonium.

Ekarto walked up to the mountain, looking at his best friend, Ayron, who was also going to go up the mountain with him. Ayron had never heard of Eldonville but going on a mountain trip is fun when your best friend is with you. And climbing this mountain wasn't going to be so hard. After all, Ayron just had to fly up. He was born with the power of air, so he could simply fly up. Ekarto was born with fire which would give him a serious boost in going up the mountain, but he wanted to climb the mountain himself. After all, how often do you get to climb a mountain to a semi-fictional kingdom?

"This is going to be so cool. Going up a mountain and then entering a kingdom that I've never heard of? That's the type of adventure I like!" Ayron exclaimed.

"Well, you better make sure you don't fall off – oh, wait."

"EXACTLY. I CAN FLY UP THIS HUGE ROCK. Why must you forget that I have the power of air? For starters, I'm wearing these epic robes, which clearly have air symbols on them."

"Okay, calm down you big baby. So, for the last time, are you ready?" Ekarto asked, a slight trail of confidence in his voice.

"You bet I am, you cow!"

"Hey. I'm not a cow."

"I know you aren't. JUST LIKE I'M NOT BORN WITH FIRE, I'M BORN WITH AIR." Ayron jabbed at Ekarto's arm, painfully enough to make Ekarto wince at the pain and brush off the imaginary bruise.

"Okay, that tells me you are ready. Somehow" Ekarto and Ayron glowed, their eyes turning white and orange. They readied themselves, taking deep breaths as the seconds went by. Then, when a crow squawked above them, almost pooping on them, they went up like lightning.

Ekarto was gripping onto the toughest rocks he could find and kept giving himself boosts and landing himself on rougher rocks, a bit of a cheating trick. If he couldn't find enough rock, he'd fly up to the nearest place to hold on to. Then he'd continue climbing.

As Ayron was soaring rapidly up the mountain, he could hear a weeping man. He was continuously weeping and crying the words, "My child!"

Ayron picked up his pace when he heard the cry but Ekarto knew better. He warned Ayron about this but Ayron was known for not being able to remember what he ate just a second ago, so he was in danger. A *lot* of danger.

As Ayron flew up the mountain, he saw to his horror that the weeping man was not indeed weeping, nor was it a man. It was a troll. They cried and wept until someone or something came to them and then crushed and ate them. Perhaps that was one reason the villagers didn't allow Ekarto to climb for so long? Well, whatever the reason was, he didn't have time to think about the infinite reasons why he wasn't allowed. Ayron was near the peak and if he wasn't close enough to the troll, it would hypnotise him to bring him closer. Ekarto started to climb vigorously with great speed, but a sudden wave of exhaustion hit him. His muscles ached and his eyelids felt heavy. His energy was drained. He was only climbing for a few minutes! Then it hit him. Another myth was that these trolls could slow down others nearby in case they would break the spell and stop the troll. The trolls were perilous enemies who would stay in places like rivers and forests. But the mountain was clear of rivers and forests. Why was there a troll here all of a sudden?

Ekarto realised that Ayron was already there as he heard a scream, followed by a weird, deep voice speaking a language Ekarto did not know of. Ekarto started to give up on climbing and flew up the mountain with the power of fire, covering his ears as he flew up.

Once he reached the top, he saw Ayron floating towards the troll. It was a purple, loathly beast. It had huge warts covering its back and had bones shooting out of its arms and legs. Its eyes were all yellow and slightly bleeding. Ekarto ran to the troll, kicking its face and snapping Ayron to his senses by slapping him and shaking him aggressively. Once Ayron came back to his senses, he started screaming for his life.

"WHERE AM I? WHAT IS THAT THING? WHY AM I HERE AND WHY IS MY CHEEK HURTING—"

"SHUSH, AYRON! WE HAVE TO MAKE THIS THING RUN!" Ayron kept blasting air at the troll and Ekarto punched flames and waved branches at it, making the troll scared, whimpering for its dear life. Ekarto looked deep into its eyes and saw that the troll was truly scared. He couldn't put his finger on it but it reminded him of his own fear, yet he remembered his whole life to be perfect and good. He threw away the branch with fire on it and let the troll escape. It was mumbling as it left, thumping its feet as it rushed through the green landscapes and the few trees surrounding the area. Ayron ran to Ekarto, confused.

"Well, the troll is gone. But not the way I had it in my head. I thought of an epic battle between man and troll, the battle between *good and evil!*"

"We got rid of only one. This might just be the beginning of whatever might happen next."

Ayron started to ponder over his decision of coming with Ekarto, but decided to leave it and continue finding Eldonville. As long as he had Ekarto, he was safe.

Ekarto shook his head and walked slowly on a single path where he could see aged arrows and eroded helmets, perhaps from a previous battle. There were vines shooting from the ground and wrapping around some weapons and old skeletons, looking as if they were trying to escape the vines from wrapping around them like a snake. It was a grim view. Then he saw an inscription on the ground:

"Eldonville is no more."

The Path

"What do you mean Eldonville is no more? We just went all that way to find a lost civilisation? Unbelievable! Ayron, this is a complete utter disgrace."

Ayron slapped Ekarto on his face, turning it slightly red. He looked quite happy yet stern, something you wouldn't see too often on Ayron.

"You really are a blind person, like when you were born." Ayron pointed east where they could see a blurry, yellow wall. It was like a rectangle and it had tall things coming out of it. And it had red things on top of the taller yellow things. He couldn't believe it.

It was Eldonville!

Ekarto started to hug Ayron, jump around like a kangaroo and sang merry tunes as he ran to the castle. It was impossible to imagine! This civilisation, he thought wasn't even real, was truly in front of his eyes! The path seemed more vibrant, more beautiful and more lush! He could see the watchtowers grow in size and if he could recall correctly, they would puff out smoke and wave red flags to alert the kingdom that there was a new arrival. And, surely, that is what they did. He waved his hands and screamed his greetings at them and they laughed and watched in astonishment. Why would anyone be so happy to come to Eldonville? They rang a huge bell, and even though it hurt Ekarto's ears, he didn't react. He kept breathing the air around him and observed the landscapes. Then he came to the front gate of Eldonville, where there were huge statues and colossal structures, massive flags flapping in the wind. He cautiously walked towards the main door, big and old, tapestries and old carvings decorated on it, flags and people telling tales no words can speak. Pictures could tell things no words had the courage to say, he had always thought.

He was in disbelief. His dreams had come true! He thought his goal to come to Eldonville would never be fulfilled, but it was fulfilled.

And now, his life would change.

Eldonville

The doors opened at once. The bolts were really rusty, so the guards found it very hard to open the door.

"Welcome to the Imperial Constitution of the Royal Eldonvillian Palace."

"Hello! I'm Ekarto, from the Silk Village." The guard's jaw dropped, his eyes widening.

"I don't believe it! It's Ekarto! He's finally here!" The guard had a mammoth of a grin on his face, and it remained as he looked at Ayron. "I don't know who you are but I surely know Ekarto! Did you know I was there at your birth? Your little feet were just kicking at us, I remember it. You were so powerful when you were just born and now you're as strong and formidable as your father was. Come in, don't be shy! Your uncle would love to meet you after all these years of separation." Ekarto and Ayron were bewildered as they walked in – how did the guards know who Ekarto was? It was quite weird but once they glimpsed around the city, their weird feelings faded away. There was a huge, ornate tower right next to them, heavily decorated with tiny, tiny sculptures carved into the outer walls. There were magnificent mansions on one side but little, wooden huts on the other. The mansions were beautifully decorated with golden tiles on the roofs, with eye-catching drawings of spirits carved into the doors. The streets were packed with people dressed in fancy clothes and funny-looking shoes. There was also a centrepiece to the village, showing a statue of a person wearing magnificent clothes, waving a staff and crushing skulls with his bare hands. The huts were tiny, filled with slime, packed with spiders and housed prisoners walking with chains on their feet and arms. On the other side were the markets with merchants waiting to spill their goods to the people and spoil the children with sweets as the villagers looked for the excellent bargain. Guards walked around, brandishing silver swords and carrying heavy shields, looking proud as they walked. The kingdom was filled with people gifted with a variety of powers, some with fire, some with life and death, some with demonic summoning, some with water, earth, air, blood, metal, sand, space and legendary powers not known to man for so long. Then they came to the greatest part of the kingdom – the palace.

It was a ginormous fortress surrounded with guards and watchtowers, flags raising the Crest of the Royal Family, which for some reason looked familiar to Ekarto. Maybe it was in one of the drawings back at the Silk Village? The palace had a great variety of buildings and halls, wings and sectors. It was a mammoth compared to the drawings Ekarto had seen in Silk Village, depicting the Eldonvillian Palace.

Ekarto and Ayron tried to sink in the view, but it was too amazing. As they were strolling to their rooms, a woman appeared, wearing a guard's uniform and had a golden emblem forged into her chest plate. "Hello there, my name is Zaula. I'm the Head Guard of the Gates. I received an order to take you to a room in the palace as it looks like you don't have an accommodation. Follow me." They walked with this woman named Zaula to the palace, which had a colossal field in front of it, with statues, flags and buildings unknown to Ekarto. Ekarto saw a wooden bed made from twigs, logs and some fabrics.

They continued to walk, but Zaula stopped dead in her tracks and glared at Ayron, who was staring.

"You creep me out."

"I wasn't staring at you. I was staring at him." Zaula turned around to see who Ayron was talking about. It was the king of Eldonville. He was wearing a strange robe, as if he were a wizard, had red eyes, hair as black as the night sky and teeth that were quite sharp. His nails were long and menacing and he wore weird shoes. He had a sword wrapped around his waist, a symbol of pride, valour and might. As soon as he saw Ekarto, he ran over to meet him.

"Greetings, greetings! Welcome to my kingdom. I was told by the guards you had returned after so long. of course I couldn't keep you waiting – I had to meet you instantly! And who are you, young man?"

"I'm Ayron, Ekarto's friend. Who are you-"

"And let's see here!" The king looked up and down at Ekarto, noticing his red ribbon on his bun. "You have the power of fire, just like me! It's surely a nice thing to meet you two. Zaula, I trust you are taking them to their rooms?"

"Yes, my King."

"Wait, we're not here for long-"

"Splendid. Well, I won't hold you any longer. Carry on then!" The king shook Ekarto's hand and then proceeded to rush to the Royal House. Ekarto thought he was weird but he didn't think about it as Zaula kept walking them to their house. And when they reached, they saw in front of them a great house built with golden roof corners pointing out of all four corners of the roof. The roof had red tiles painting it red and had a rather impressive arch looming over the door with a spirit carved onto it. It was a fire spirit wearing a hat. Ekarto also thought he had seen him somewhere before but he was too tired to think. When Zaula opened the doors, Ayron ran around, screaming with joy and threw himself onto the master bed in one of the dozen bedrooms. Ekarto just walked to the nearest bedroom and slumped onto a bed, closing his eyes. He didn't know why but a sudden drowsiness overcame him. And at once, he fell into a heavy sleep.

The City of Eldon

Ekarto walked out of the front door, quite nervous about how the people were going to be compared to the people in Silk Village. He expected people to maybe stare at him, perhaps ask him questions or give some tour around town. But people continued on with their daily lives. Ekarto breathed in, then breathed out. He started advancing to the main town, which was only a few yards away. Ayron was sprinting and laughing around the town centre, excited to make some friends.

Ekarto first saw an old lady sweeping the floor, whilst her husband (or what seemed to be her husband) was fixing the sign of a bakery. They looked quite miserable. Then something caught Ekarto's attention. A picture of a man. He seemed younger than the old couple and had the picture of a woman next to it. There was also a picture of three babies and on top of that family, there was the picture of the spirit of death. There was a death wreath and a funeral wreath on the pictures and were the words:

"You fought valiantly, Munbo, and died with honour on the battlefield. Rest in Peace, Munbo Ka Lee, for you will never be forgotten."

It was a heart-breaking passage and beside the whole death memorial were two candles with smoke drifting away in the breeze. Ekarto walked up to them and the old lady looked up at him, confused.

"Well, er, hello. I'm Ekarto, just a new guy around town. Nice to meet you. I'm terribly sorry for what happened to Munbo. I send my condolences," he said, terrified of the lady's eyes, which reminded him of snakes for some reason.

"Hello, young man. I've been waiting for your arrival for 23 years. 23 long, long years. And look at you! You're all grown up and manly. You know when you were born, I was one of the clerics? I can still remember your snoring! It was cute. And thank you for your condolences. Would you like to have some sweets?" She opened a box full of Forest sweets, which Ekarto had never seen before and it was actually quite surprising to see such little, round and vibrant colours of sweets, all caged in a small box, ready to be eaten. Ekarto reluctantly picked up a sweet and ate it, nervous of what impression he would give off to the old lady. But when the taste kicked in, he was really enjoying them! He fed some to Ayron, who was quite sad that he, in fact, did not make any new friends up to now.

Ekarto kept strolling around the city. He was amazed at how historic the city was, with statues and memorials to past monarchs, and a towering statue of a man with an unusual crown. Inscriptions read he was the first king of Eldonville, Eldon himself. Ekarto felt happy when looking at the statue. He didn't know why, but he felt he had a connection to Eldon.

He continued to walk around town until a house caught his eye. He walked over to the house, which was separated from all the other houses. This time, he met a young, desolate woman, whose hair was red and looked like blood.

"Uh, hello there? I'm Ekarto. How are you today?" he said with a trail of fear in his voice.

"I'm fine," she wearily said as if she had just done a long day of work and needed rest. "You're one of the first people to care about us. Usually, people don't mind how much we have to work and toil to make sure they can be fed." Ekarto saw as the woman examined his eyes and his clothes. He eventually realised she was trying to find out his power.

"I have the power of fire. What were you born with?"

"Figure it out yourself." She mindlessly crushed sugarcanes and cut fruit and vegetables up into tiny pieces as she put them into a clay bowl. There were many clay bowls filled with fruits and vegetables behind her. How long had she been doing this for?

Ekarto looked at the woman's hands, which had drawings of a spirit. It had red specks of paint around the spirit. It hit him – this woman was born with the power of blood.

"You were gifted with the power of blood," Ekarto excitedly said. But then he frowned a bit. What if the woman was planning to kill Ekarto?

"My name is Indra of Kuzutama, a place you might have not heard about. I was captured by your uncle and his army, separated from my home and my family. I was put in this dump and now work as a sugar cane farmer and have to cut up fruits and vegetables for the rich. I used to be the richest girl in my town but now I'm the poorest. I was able to stop the soldiers from getting me and taking me in a chariot full of prisoners but the king simply grabbed a staff and somehow stopped me from using my powers." She quickly stared into

Ekarto's eyes, a glimmer of hope shining brightly in her, mixed with a trail of doubt. "Can you help me? You can and you can't. You can because you have the power. But you can't because you know nothing and are too inexperienced. Well, train quickly. The kingdom needs you and always did." Ekarto was now beyond baffled. Who was she talking about? His uncle didn't have an army, he didn't even know who his uncle was! Only the old man back at Silk Village that would aggressively shake his hand and chew leaves. He was quite pale to be Ekarto's uncle, but he didn't think much about it. Uncle Bobby, they called him.

"Wait, who and what? My mind is going crazy." The girl smiled, then the sky turned grey and dreamy. Ekarto saw a man in the sky, who looked similar to him. The same jawline, the same eyebrows, the same eyes. He was smiling down to Ekarto, and Ekarto strangely felt safe around him. Comforted by the warm smile. The man was wearing a crown on his head.

The very same the king had put on yesterday.

But then he heard a faint, distant scream from the stranger and a vision of him lying on the ground, blood soaking his clothes. Then his last vision appeared. A person in the shadows laughing with a trail of evil in his voice, a bloody dagger in his hand and a long, twisted staff.

Leaftor's Revelation

The sky turned blue again. No one seemed to care about it, as if no one had actually *seen* it. They were just chatting, working, studying, playing and so on. But Ekarto was dumbstruck. Who was the man with the dagger? Why was the man lying on the floor, bleeding? Why wasn't there an answer to this? Ekarto breathed in deeply, then let it all out. He had a thought. Who could give him answers? Then he had one option in his head. He went to the King's chamber to see if he knew anything. But then he hesitated. First of all, it might be disrespectful to disturb the King. Secondly, the King had a staff, and the murderer had a staff. Was there any connection? And lastly, the King was in the bathroom, as some guards told him. So Ekarto walked around the corridors for a little while when he saw a door that had a leaf carved into it. Ekarto somehow felt a link to the door and then knocked, slightly opening the door. There was a spiralling staircase that went down a dark room. Ekarto was slightly scared, but he remembered fire gave off light, and he had the power of fire! So, he created a flame in his palm and walked down.

The room was supposedly large, as every step Ekarto took could echo for quite some time as he walked. The room was void of all the light in the world, except for his flame. He could hear a rather annoying dripping noise in the distance but ignored it. Ekarto continued to walk on, and then he found some door. It was wooden, with another leaf carved into it. Ekarto didn't know why, but he had a compulsion to knock. And so, he did.

"Who's there at my door knocking?"

"Uh, I'm Ekarto. I'm new around here."

"Ekarto? Is it really you?" Ekarto could hear someone inside the room scrambling for the door. The sound of chains resonated throughout the whole room. Ekarto saw a man with a tattered green tunic open the door, his face radiant with delight.

"Oh my, come in! It really is you! You're not fake! I've been waiting for you for 23 years. Come in, come in." Ekarto nervously closed the door behind him and was once again known for being waited on for 23 years. Why was everyone waiting for him for 23 years? He was just an unknown villager from the Silk Village. That's all. But it didn't matter anymore when Ekarto saw this man's cell.

The cell was vast, mostly painted green and had maps of the world on the grey, chipped walls, painted onto sheets of linen. There were leaves all around the room as if he lived in a leafy, bushy castle. There were torches too. Next to a tank of water (showing the picture of a leaf spirit) was a bed. It was stained and heavily damaged. Then, in the centre of it all, a little tree with a variety of fruits growing on it. The ground surrounding it was cracked, with soil carelessly scattered around the hole. The man was chained, however. His arms were restrained, but the chains seemed to be loose. How else would he have opened the door? There was a rather pleasant smell of fresh crops and plants wafting around in the room. It was mixed with a light smell of rust.

Ekarto saw the man that had called him in and looked at him. He was a well-built man. He was quite tall, the same height as Ekarto. His hair was tightened up in a bun, with a metal pin going through his hair. His right eyebrow had a burn in it, and his hands were strangely red in some areas, obviously burn marks. His left eye had a scar running down it. There was single tear running down his cheek. What happened to him? Ekarto, as always, did not have time to think about this when Leaftor pulled Ekarto down to a chair and patted his shoulder.

"Well, sit down! Eat something! Loosen up a bit, you're in my cell now." Ekarto sat down, adjusted himself, and decided to get straight to the point.

"Who are you?" The man hesitated for a bit and moved in his chair uncomfortably.

"I am Leaftor. I was your father's closest friend. We have known each other since childhood."

"My father's friend?"

"Oh, I haven't told you yet."

"Told me what?"

"I'll tell you later. So, how'd you know I was here?"

"I didn't. I just walked in here."

"Fate is ever so good." Leaftor bowed down his head towards Ekarto and looked up to the sky. Then he looked at Ekarto.

"Do you know by any chance about a vision in the sky?"

"I'm sorry, what?"

"A vision! A man in a crown stabbed on the floor, a maniac with a staff and dagger laughing in the night, what in the daylights was I seeing?" Leaftor looked very uncomfortable.

"Come here then. I'll tell you everything, right from the beginning. I can sense you've been travelling a lot and met a few people including me of course. I'll tell you everything."

"Well, tell me. Who was the man in the vision?"

"What you saw wasn't any old person. It was your father."

"Wait a hot second. My father is back at Silk Village! Oh, no, is he dead?"

"No, you innocent thing. That guy back in Silk Village isn't your father." Ekarto just felt a sense of shock that shot up his spine. If that man back at the village wasn't his father, who was? Who was he? Who was Ekarto? Was Ekarto even his real name?

"Who am I then? Who are you? Who is my father? My family? My uncle? Why has everyone waited for 23 years for me? EXPLAIN."

"Ekarto, it's going to take me a long time to explain but let me get straight to the point. Your father's name was Okarto and he was once going to be the king of Eldonville. Your uncle is Okoto, who is the present King. You have a mother named Okinara. And the reason why everyone has waited for you for 23 years is purely because you had to escape from Okoto. You are the prince of Eldonville." Ekarto had butterflies in his tummy. He was a prince? His father was once about to become a King? The present king was his uncle? He actually has royal blood? He couldn't believe it.

He was holding his hands against his head, obviously shocked from the news. He really didn't come from Silk Village? He came from here? He was slightly sad but he was quite happy too. His home was a ginormous palace! He did feel better once he realised this but the shock still remained.

"Leaftor, why did I have to escape from Okoto?"

"I will explain it all. And with that, you need to know the story of your father too."

The Tando Ingots

"We will start when Okarto and Okoto were just teens, when their father, Ukarto, was already dead for almost three years. Ukarto died from a mysterious disease, the clerics called Mibortin from the Bidelite word 'Mirtin', which means deadly. You shouldn't know much about Bideli, so I won't bore you with that. Your grandmother, Urkata, raised her two sons by herself, Okarto as the apple of her eye. He was strong, smart and wise, always making sure his family was safe and learnt the ways of the monarchs of Eldonville when he learnt he could be the new king of Eldonville. Okoto, well, he was also strong and smart but he was quite clumsy. He'd often forget things, knock items over, stay up late and wake up late, you get it. Urkata was one day testing the two brothers on the month of Kaarzinan, a month in the Eldonvillian calendar where the heirs to the throne would be tested to see how able they were to lead such a massive nation. On the first day of Kaarzinan, they started their test – finding the Tando Ingots.

"The Tando Ingots were a special family of metal. Not only were they naturally quite purple but they were alive. They were some of the most troublesome creatures in the realm, accidentally created by a madman named Himada. He poured some potion on them to make them more valuable or something, I don't have a clue about that story. But what's truly important, Ekarto, is that they were the hardest things to find in the Kingdom. Now, I'm sure you've seen the palace and the city. It's ginormous. So how could they possibly find something like this? And what kind of test was this? It was a test to see if they could find things impossible to find. An example could be criminals or jewellery or some books. The list goes on! However I still question the point of the test.

"Okarto and Okoto were stationed at the steps of the Royal Palace, where they were signalled to start finding the Tando Ingots. Okoto lost hope in the mission already but he wearily tried looking, mocked by his subjects for being too lazy. He just sulkily walked to his mother, who hugged him and comforted him. I wasn't able to hear properly but I think she said something like, 'There are four other tests left and 29 days left of this month, so you will win. Kill the Elephant and fly to Stenland, the pigeons will eat your cows…' Yeah. I couldn't hear properly.

"Okarto was sprinting around the houses of the Kingdom, the houses the Ingots would normally be. They would just mess around and knock things over until they were bored and move on to the next house. And to Okarto's disappointment, the whole Kingdom was messed up by the Ingots. He started to give up but even though he'd win for being so resilient for the longest period of time, he still kept running until he couldn't run anymore. Then, he came up with an idea.

"He remembered that the Ingots were attracted to clumsiness, foolishness, craziness and madness. Himada himself was a madman, as I said earlier, so they would probably be pulled by a large force of such ridiculousness. So, Okarto thought of the maddest thing of all – to dress up as a woman and start dancing and chanting like a mental donkey. He quickly grabbed some clothes, fashioned his face with some paste and chalk, grabbed some bells and started to dance and chant. He was extremely embarrassed but he kept doing so, even when the people laughed at him. His own mother was ashamed to look at him. And for nearly six minutes, there was no response.

"I don't know how and I don't exactly remember it well but after a few minutes of his chanting, there were sudden rumbles in the ground. Small pebbles, large pottery, tall poles, short cups, all fell to the ground. There was a massive cloud of dust coming his way and to his surprise, he saw the Ingots speeding past to reach Okarto. He chanted and chanted until they reached him and he grabbed a net and caught the ingots, nearly burning the net with such intensity. He walked to his mother with his feet swollen and bruised from his walking and put the Ingots to sleep."

"Oh my, did my dad kill them?"

"No! He literally put them to sleep. I don't think you can kill metal. They were quietly snoring and the miners of Eldonville safely transported the ingots to the mines where they were found. They may be used again, maybe for your own sons and daughters. That would be nice.

"Urkata was very proud, I could tell. She announced happily that Okarto was the victor of the test. Other tests also had Okarto as the brother that would win the test. Okoto didn't win a single one. Okarto was extremely pleased and was promoted to the Minister of the Kingdom in between the Prime Minister and the Monarch. Although it was a joyous occasion for Okarto, Okoto was filled with rage and anger. I still have doubts about it, but I believe he was possessed by a chaotic spirit, and still is to this day."

Ekarto's Mother

"Is that why I had to run away?" Ekarto asked.

"Well, we're not there yet."

"Ugh, this is so long." Ekarto complained. He rolled his eyes and rested his head on his hands, blowing his hair away. Leaftor chuckled and told Ekarto.

"This part of the story you'd find interesting, believe me."

Leaftor stopped speaking for a while and drank some water. Ekarto was quite tired but intrigued. Leaftor started munching on some Sun Fruits – the fruit that would give energy, memory and wisdom (as told by the merchants, that is). It was shaped like a banana but it was quite crunchy and had a thick layer of solidified sap. The sap was green, which would fool any scavenging animal to think it was a poisonous fruit. But under the green sap was a golden fruit, soft and glossy from being in sap for too long. This was the sweet and tangy part Leaftor loved, similar to a strawberry. It had orange stripes on its thin skin and circles that looked like stars glimmering in the night sky. Leaftor's hands and mouth were all sticky from the sap and Ekarto snickered as he thought Leaftor looked like a little baby learning to eat! Leaftor washed his hands and faced and returned to his chair, ready to resume the story.

"All right. Let's start again. Where were we? Oh, those fruits were nice…"

"You were going on about Dad's victory and Okoto's evil thing."

"Ah, yes. Anyway, we have dealt with the teenager-hood of your dad. Now, let's move onto the main part of this." Leaftor then did a massive burp, slamming his hands against his chest like a gorilla to let it all out. It looked quite gross to Ekarto but one side of him thought he was a funny man. Maybe that was just how men thought. That would be what his mother would tell him. Back in the village, not here.

"Excuse me. Let's start properly this time. We can now fast forward around 12 years later when Okarto was 23 years old. He was about to be coronated but in order for this to happen, he had to find a wife quickly. It was a royal custom to do so except for Eldon as he, well, created the kingdom without the wife. Okarto went around the kingdom, looking and searching for the perfect one. Many people offered their girls to become the Queen of Eldonville, either to inherit the money and become rich or to send their daughters away for good. Okarto rejected them all and went to extreme lengths. He even searched around the whole country! Unluckily, his search was unsuccessful. Just then he thought of the wildest idea ever. To go to Swanlonalville.

"Swanlonalville was Eldonville's arch enemy. Simply because it waged many wars with Eldonville, either side winning or losing. It had a ridiculous backstory and copied Eldon's mission of spreading peace and stability to the world. Swanlonalville was miniscule compared to Eldonville, but it was still very rich and powerful. I once had to eat a swan when I went visiting there. It tasted awful.

"I wasn't there when he went to Swanlonalville, so I can't really say what happened. But after two days of searching, he returned in a big chariot pulled by him. He was pulling his wife home! Of course, they weren't married yet, so…anyways. He reached the steps of the palace and out came a woman named Marika. She was a noble woman, the daughter of a rich landlord who was looking for a good man. Okarto assumed a fake identity and the landlord liked Okarto's personality, something like that. I can't recall very well. Apparently, they met when there was a huge sale of fruit and they both got the same exact fruits, same exact number! They started chatting and before you know it, they're at Eldonville. I don't think Marika was expecting Okarto to bring her to Eldonville but she seemed so happy. Okarto was the happiest of all, as if it was his coronation on that day. And, well, it was very soon.

"Queen Urkata wasn't so happy. After all, she hated anyone from Swanlonalville. She was really eager for an Eldonvillian bride, even if it was a poor woman from the soils of Eldonville. She only really cared if the woman was from Eldonville, not if the future Queen was dumb, mute, deaf or a tyrannical and corrupt soul. All that mattered was that she was Eldonvillian. But she put her grudges aside as Marika walked up to her and greeted her with utmost respect, calling her 'Majestic and Noble Queen'. No one ever gave her titles like this, so she was happy with the relationship to continue. But, unfortunately, Okoto was still controlled by the same spirit. And he was determined to become King. Well, that's what I think at least.

"Their marriage happened very quickly and, surprisingly, it was quite boring. There were nice decorations but it was grey and dull, held in a funeral hall. Urkata was out in the country, so Okoto held the marriage. He kept throwing dead petals at them and gifted them absolutely useless things like chicken feathers and other garbage. But if I didn't see it, I wouldn't believe it for Okarto and Marika were extremely happy on such a day, even if it was so quick and dull. They just exchanged vows, prayed, blessed each other, received gifts and that was all. Around a few minutes or so. And when the marriage finished, everyone returned home and there was no mention of it until the Queen returned after a week. She heard of how Okoto conducted the marriage and obviously scolded him like any mother would. Okoto became furious and a week later he decided he was going to kill Okarto for 'stepping into his way of glory'. I don't know how any of that was stepping into his way of glory, but that's what a vision told me in my sleep. I'll trust it.

"Now, Okoto and Okarto were very loving brothers. They never really fought and understood how much their mother had gone through when King Ukarto died. So, they always protected her and made sure she was fine and well, both physically and mentally. But Okoto, blinded with rage, couldn't control the chaos spirit in him and plotted his way of killing my very best friend. And believe me, he had it very well planned.

"It was a few months later after the marriage and Okarto was going to be coronated. Okoto loathed this day and it was now upon him. It was his decision to either kill him now or later or never. And he wanted to torture Okarto before his death and he knew just how.

"Okoto rushed down the Royal Halls to the Queen's chamber, where I was talking to Urkata about the economy, as we do. He was panting and told Urkata the worst lie I had ever heard. He said that Okarto was plotting to overthrow the monarchy, kill the higher council and imprison us all. He said the idea of power got into his head or something.

"Urkata thought that this was all lies but I could see she was deeply worried. After all, Okarto was powerful and why would Okoto be so upset and nervous? Then, he said something even worse.

"He was planning to sabotage the throne and let Swanlonalville take the throne for his love of Marika. Marika had apparently manipulated him for the throne.

"Now, this seemed quite believable to Urkata and even to me, who was a foolish man at that time. He did seem to let Marika do anything she pleased and even celebrated the Swan Festivals that no Eldonvillian ever celebrated! Urkata ordered that on his coronation, he must be given a trial. And he might have to give up his wife to make sure she doesn't allow Swanlonalville to share the throne as she had the power to do so as the Queen.

"After a few hours, we met Okarto wearing some robes that his father would've worn when he was coronated. He kissed the stone of his father's grave and greeted his mother. She had to pretend that she wasn't suspicious, so she also greeted him too. I was confident that Okarto was all pure and had good intentions but a part of me felt that I had to stick with reality – Okarto might become a traitor after all. He sat at the mini throne, where the coronation would take place and everyone started to pile up in the hall, waiting for the Priests to come with the Crowns and other gifts of the Throne.

"Urkata sat on her throne and watched the coronation take place. She was happy for Okarto but she was also immensely petrified of what could happen, should Okarto take full power. He was about to be anointed with some water from the springs when Urkata stopped the anointing. She claimed that Okarto would have to choose between his wife and the throne, because Marika would allow Swanlonalville to take power. Okarto and Marika looked confused and Urkata even accused Okarto of not changing Marika's name to something similar to Okarto's name. Out of the blue, I blurted out that Marika's new name could be Okinara. I was going to ask Okarto if he liked it or not, but in the situation, I couldn't ask for anyone's opinions."

"I like it."

"Thank you, Ekarto. The arguments stopped for a while and it seemed that I saved the day. Sort of.

"Urkata accepted the name but still scolded Okarto for not thinking of a name. So far it seemed Okoto was angry that his plan wasn't working. And then he raised his voice at Okarto for apparently injuring him throughout his life and making fun of him for not being strong enough. Urkata believed him, blinded by Okoto's lies and fear for the throne, and somehow Okoto was very prepared for this. He learnt magic from before and created an illusion in everyone's heads of Okarto laughing at Okoto and punching him to see if Okoto was strong enough to defend himself. Everyone was shocked but some were adamant on the fact that Okarto didn't do this. This wasn't real or it was taken out of context. I too believed this was fake but Urkata was believing every little thing that she saw. Urkata was furious at Okarto and declared he was not fit for the throne. Many of the advisors and high ministers argued that this was happening without any proper reason, and none of the accusations had anything to do with Okarto becoming the King. Things became worse when Urkata threw a dagger at a minister's neck, and demanded silence. Everyone was terrified of Urkata, even Okoto. Okoto tried to reassure his mother, but even he was pushed away from his own mother. Urkata and Okoto may have the same view of Okarto not taking the throne, but Urkata was not going to deal with Okoto. Then she asked Okarto to be banished with Okinara from the palace or that there be a divorce and Okoto is crowned King. Okoto gleamed when he heard this and Okarto accepted the banishment, albeit reluctantly. Either way, Okoto would become King. On that day, Ekarto, your parents were banished from Eldonville."

Okarto Is Dead

Leaftor stopped for a bit as Ekarto's eyes started to fill up with tears. Leaftor could understand why and he heard Ekarto panted angrily, hearing as Okoto was laughing above with some people. His fists clenched but he restrained himself.

"Carry on, Leaftor."

"Very well, then. Are you sure you can take this all in?"

"I'll have to."

"All right then. Let's continue. Okarto and Okinara and me."

"Wait, you went with them too?"

"Yes. Of course, I was Okarto's best friend. I needed to accompany him. So I went out of the palace with him and looked back at its amazing glory for the last time. Okarto and Okinara and I were stripped off our jewellery, clothes and wore villager clothes from then on. And we walked over to the nearest village – Silk Village. We wanted to be close to the city."

Ekarto couldn't believe what he was hearing. His parents and Leaftor lived where he was living his whole life? Unbelievable! Next, he might've said that Okarto had the same voice as Ekarto.

"Did you know, Ekarto, that your voice is very similar to Okarto's? I just never really mentioned it until now."

Astonishing.

"We were accepted into the Silk Village and although it took a bit of time to get used to the village life, we helped build the village. Okarto was chosen to be a council member of the Silk Village and decided their military tactics and how to defend the village. I heard that on the same day Okarto became a council member, Okoto was crowned to become King. Urkata was sad and desolate but Okoto was so happy he forgot to celebrate with his own mother, who needed some cheering up, I believe. And I feared this day because when I knew how much he hated Okarto and how much power he had now, it would've only been a matter of minutes until something went horribly wrong.

"The next day, when Okinara and Okarto were helping out with cleaning their house, we heard trumpets come from the entrance of Eldonville and we saw a battalion of guards marching towards the village with Okoto being carried in a palanquin. The Silk Army had assembled and got out their weapons and cried battle chants in case the Eldonvillians were here to attack. But they dropped their weapons when the army stopped dead in their tracks and Okoto came forward, no guards with him. He was smiling and carrying bags. He said hello to Okarto and went on about how he was sorry for the banishment. Truly, he was not. He threw dead flowers over them again, like in their wedding and gave them even more useless gifts. Then he announced he would stay here for a bit. Okarto, who was probably on the brink of madness, stomped on the ground and scowled at Okoto, who was still smirking. He then said that Okoto would one day regret the day he became king. Okoto's army started to advance, and then Okarto breathed fire at the sky and directed it at Okoto's army. They cowered back, some burnt by the flames. Okoto ran back and ordered that the army detained Okarto but he was still breathing fire. The Silk Army chased off the Eldonvillian army. Okoto looked back at us, sweating with fear.

"Okarto dropped himself on his bed, crying immensely. He told me he couldn't believe he had to resort to this and felt very guilty. I can't explain how sad he was. He dearly loved Okoto but Okoto hated him back. He kept asking why he was meant to go through this and kept crying until he was left with no more tears and walked out of his hut, cooking for his village with Okinara.

"On the next day, he decided to help the village improve their economy because they had become very poor from taxes and their army funds. He created businesses and markets, established a trading company that would do dealings and trades with other nations that would give the Silk Village a massive boost to their treasury's supply in money. He also exported Silk to rich customers as the Silk Village was renowned for its magnificent silk and fabrics, hence the name of the village. Okarto turned Silk Village into Silk City! He made it a very powerful city in which the rich would live in for a good life of business and peace. But it wouldn't stay like that forever, Ekarto. And I'm sure you know what it looks like now." Ekarto nodded, reminiscing the village in his head. It was just made up of a few wooden huts, a town hall made from rubble and a poor school with rarely any books or money. He could start imagining what his father did with the village. Ekarto smiled as he thought of it. Leaftor also smiled and remembered what he could still hold on to about the city. It was a vast landscape in his time and now, he didn't know.

"A few days later, I heard that some nobles of the kingdom were coming to Silk City for refuge as Okoto was starting an Empire for Eldonville. He already took over the Kingdom of Swanlonalville and was starting to take over Cabourice and Dastirao's States. He also united Eldonville and made it more centralised. Now all of Eldonville's citizens were bound by Okoto's law and reign, and all the armies were unified.

"Silk City was the place where people could escape from Okoto's army, who had taken every citizen in the capital and made them workers for the Kingdom's army. Okarto was deeply scared and he was even more terrified when he heard his mother was imprisoned for trying to shut down the Empire and scolding Okoto or now known as Emperor Okoto. The Silk Army was fully alert and was preparing for the day Okoto and the Silk City would go to war. And it wasn't too far away.

"One day, your mother became pregnant with you, during the Conquest of Eldonville trying to fight the nearby Forest Kingdom. Okarto was eager to see his baby son born and the city was becoming more and more rich, preparing a Royal Hospital just for you to be born in. The city was so rich it could build anything it wanted, just because it could. Okoto was even preparing for your birth and was somehow excited for your birth. The citizens of the Silk City were hoping you and Okarto would take back Eldonville and rise to power again but it wouldn't happen like they wanted it to.

"On the day of your birth, a messenger was coming to the city to alert Okarto of more nobles who were lucky to escape Eldonville. Okarto had to leave Okinara so he could show the nobles some homes they would have preferred to stay in and then another messenger said Okoto would like Ekarto's birth to happen at the palace. The Silk clerics, while they didn't want to, moved Okinara out of her home and speedily rushed her to the palace, as she was starting to deliver. Okarto was sad he couldn't witness your birth but what happened next was absolutely horrifying. It was grim. Brutal. I don't know if you can even listen at this point-"

"JUST TELL ME ALREADY!" Ekarto shrieked. Leaftor coiled back but he wasn't scared. Just shocked. Ekarto looked sorry and Leaftor forgave him by patting him on the head. Ekarto let him carry on.

"The nobles, who had come to the city, told your father that they were hearing weird noises from the forests of Silk City and their child was lost too. Okarto thought he should go into the forests to investigate and indeed he heard weird noises. But when he arrived, it was no creature he was expecting. It was Okoto and he looked very ill and inhumane, cracks of blood appearing in his face. That's what I heard from a witness before she disappeared but after Okarto saw Okoto in that state, he asked if he was alright apparently. Okoto laughed and the 'nobles' held his arms tightly. It turned out these people were working for Okoto and were helping him kill Okarto. Okarto struggled and kicked his way out but they kept retaining him, their grip growing more painful by the second. Okoto took out an axe and Okarto stared at it with immense fear. Okarto pleaded with Okoto not to kill him and kept talking about their childhood and how good their relationship was. For a split second, Okoto stopped and looked confused. But then he started to act up, teeth turning bloody and sharp and screamed at Okarto. It was horrible as

Okarto was repeatedly getting slashes at his chest, mouth oozing with blood. He split your father's chest open with an axe. Okoto then held the head of Okarto and spat on it. The spies threw the body in a cave, letting it rot in there. That, Ekarto, was your father's last few minutes in this world. At least that's what the witness told me." Ekarto looked at Leaftor, desolate and scared. He looked pale and empty, his blood draining from his face. He looked around the place and wondered why his father had to undergo such a terrible death. Nothing made sense to him. *Why?* He kept asking himself.

"I know, Ekarto. I know. I was wondering where he had been for so long, and he was nowhere to be found in the city. The very same people that held Okarto as he was killed told me he was killed by a bear in a cave and pointed to the cave where his body was. I walked towards the direction of the cave, and, maybe I was wrong, but I heard distant footsteps from within. I was called by a villager as your mother had already given birth. I went there for your birth, took you and came back to the village only to see it ransacked. The Silk Army was nearly wiped out as well as the Eldonvillian Army, and Okoto arrested me. I gave you away to a woman who held you during the attacks. I think Okinara may have been arrested. She could be alive for all I know. What I do know is that after I had been arrested, I was tortured, hence the scars. I had to bathe in boiling water once to apparently 'teach me some shame' as I had scowled at Okoto as I was tortured. I was continuously whipped with both fire and leather. Then I was locked up in here, and for 23 years, I sat here in hopes you would grow up and liberate us." Leaftor's eyes started to tear up. His eyes turned red, and teardrops slowly trickled down his cheek as he remembered the pain he endured. Ekarto gently wiped the tears off, allowing Leaftor to recollect himself and continue.

"Ekarto, you must avenge your father's death and make sure my burns in the prison meant something and that they were worth it. 20 long years of prison is nothing compared to what your mother probably went through. I don't know how you will avenge my pain and your father's death, but I know you will. Avenge us all, Ekarto. You are our only hope."

Home Sweet Home

Ekarto looked dumbfounded and he was. He couldn't take this in. Leaftor understood and gave him a cup of water to drink. Ekarto drank from it and left the cell, sulking and walking as if he died on the spot. Ekarto kept remembering the words in his head, *"You are our only hope, Ekarto. You are our only hope, Ekarto. You are our only hope, Ekarto."* He shook his head and walked up the spiral staircase, this time with no flame to guide his steps. He walked out of the King's Chamber and towards Ayron.

Ekarto walked past Ayron, who was nearly asleep, and was looking out of the windows. He was tirelessly searching for Ekarto and had not eaten any food. And when he saw Ekarto, he stomped up to him happily yet angrily.

"COME ON, EKARTO. WHAT TOOK YOU SO LONG! YOU JUST SUDDENLY VANISH IN THE MIDDLE OF NOWHERE! WHAT'S WRONG WITH YOU! Anyways, I am truly happy you are home. Did you know a little baby monkey came inside the house and I carried it to its mother. It was very nice and warming, you missed it all out."

"Shush, Ayron. I want to sleep."

"WHAT? IT'S AFTERNOON! YOU CAN'T BE SLEEPING NOW! THEN WHAT? YOU'LL WAKE UP IN THE MIDDLE OF THE NIGHT ONLY TO GO ON YOUR MYSTERIOUS HIKES IN WHO KNOWS WHERE. ON MY WORD, WE WILL STAY HERE ALL AWAKE UNTIL I HEAR AN OWL." At that very moment an owl was screeching and Ekarto smiled vaguely and started walking to his bed. Ayron clenched his arm and it shocked Ekarto so much he returned to his normal state.

"AAAAAARGH! What's wrong with you, Ayron? You could've popped my arms off! Oh, I think my arm is broken, oh, no."

"No, you big baby. I was doing that to see if you could actually wake up from whatever that was!" Ekarto looked at Ayron and broke into an uncontrollable laughter. Ayron was still angry but he couldn't hold it in as Ekarto had a contagious laugh and he started to giggle with Ekarto too. All that until they sat down and carried on their usual day of tidying up the house and exploring the kingdom.

"So, Ekarto. I want to ask you why were you so pale and weird earlier? Did something happen? Possibly mosquitoes. Wait, there aren't any here."

"I'll tell you but no one should hear this or they'll throw us out." Ekarto dragged Ayron back to their house, shut the doors and windows and sat down on some chairs.

"Seems, um, interesting."

"Oh, it is." Ekarto lit up some candles to make the room look more fit to be a story-telling grotto. Something they both came across in Eldonville, which was even spookier than theirs. Ekarto didn't want to bore Ayron like Leaftor did, so he got straight to the point.

"The King. You know him?" Ekarto asked.

"Uh, yeah. That weird man with a crown. What about him?"

"He is my uncle." Ayron gasped in awe and looked excited.

"YOU'RE A PRINCE."

"Be quiet, Ayron! Do you want the world to hear?" Ayron clasped his hands over his mouth and was laughing like a toddler. Ekarto shook his head.

"Well, that's not all. My uncle is evil. My father and mother, who were supposed to inherit this throne, were banished by my grandmother, who was deceived by my uncle. Then my uncle killed my dad and imprisoned my mother. Now, I must avenge my parents," Ekarto hastily said out of breath. Ayron was gaping at Ekarto, no words coming out. His eyes were wide open as if they could seamlessly fall out of his sockets.

"Woah. That's an amazing fairy tale right there. All right, I'm going to go out now, it's still a long time before night time."

"It's not a fairy tale, Ayron! It's real! Why do you think that King's face looks all cracked and torn? It's because of his anger! Or something. I don't know!"

"Well, if he really did kill your father, why didn't he kill you? And how do you know this stuff anyway? Who told you this?"

"A friend of my father's." Ayron started laughing hysterically. He swept his hands like he saw a fly and clenched his stomach, slamming his palm against a wall. Ekarto glared at Ayron. What was so funny about that?

"A FRIEND OF YOUR FATHER'S? THAT'S ABSOLUTELY CRAZY! YOUR DAD HAS NO FRIENDS BACK AT THE VILLAGE! ABSURD! BAHAHAHAHA!" Ekarto then became infuriated and slapped Ayron on the face to calm him down.

"Thanks, I needed that."

"I'm not making this up! I know everything about my family! That family back at Silk Village isn't mine! Why do you think they wouldn't allow me to go to Eldonville? TO PROTECT ME. I'm strong now and I think Okoto's planning something."

"Who in the world is Okoto?"

"Okoto is the King's name. My uncle's name. And my father's name was Okarto. Don't you see? We have similar sounding names! If anything, there has to be a resemblance in the names! Come on, Ayron, it's too clear!" Ekarto was exhausted after arguing and walked to his room, threw himself on his bed and slept instantly. Ayron went out of the room and continued to explore Eldon's city. If Ekarto wasn't going to, then tough luck. Ayron was going to instead.

The Dream

Ekarto slept soundly in the night and didn't move a muscle as from how tired he was. He looked dead but he was just sleeping. Then he started to dream and it wasn't like any other dream he had.

He saw a blurry, lowing figure. It was red, orange and yellow. Harmonious colours. It slowly walked up to him and then the figure was clearer. It was some sort of spirit. It had a weird mark on its forehead, no legs and had a head made from flames.

"Hello, Ekarto. It's nice to see you after all these years," it spoke in a calm and deep voice, echoing and faded.

"Who are you?"

"That's not important. Listen, I only have a few minutes to say what I have to say. Do you promise to not interrupt? After all, I can answer all your questions later." Ekarto nodded and carefully listened to the spirit.

"You know what happened with your father and I know too. It was a horrible demise. Yet you can change things for your kingdom! Your ancestors tirelessly worked hard to make sure Eldonville was safe, peaceful and good. Many monarchs have tried to ruin this great country but no one could succeed without an heir to the throne, destroying evil. And evil never comes to a complete end. Ekarto, I hate to break this to you but unfortunately, you face a very powerful tyrant. No tyrant for over 300 years has ever created a powerful empire such as this and it's only in your power to defeat Okoto and wake the world up from its slumber. No country or kingdom is willing to face Eldonville. I see the fire burning in your heart to do good, so use it. When opportunity comes, it is only up to you to make sure you either take it or leave it. Every second of your life cannot ever be returned, so isn't it better to take all the chances you have? You will be taken to the Forest Kingdom, a mighty continental country that is always looking out for Eldonville. It has faced great pillaging and war but has emerged victorious. There, you will meet many people who will help you in going to an ancient city called Vragos in the Imperial Fire Tribes. Over there you have to release some spirits who have been trapped in stone longer than I can remember. If you succeed, you will be given great rewards and after that you have to gather a great army to fight Okoto and take the throne. Everyone is willing to fight but they are scared and it is that fear that will let time pass by out of their own control. You have to do this, Ekarto, or the world will be taken over by Okoto. But first, release the spirits. They will protect you in the future."

"Wait, how will I go to the Forest Kingdom?"
"You're already there."

The Forest Kingdom

Ekarto instantly woke up, rubbing his head as though he were sleeping on a stone slab in the middle of nowhere. And he was sleeping on a stone slab in the middle of nowhere along with Leaftor, Zaula, Ayron, a princess from some kingdom (obviously) and a bandit from who knows where. Everyone else woke up, also rubbing their heads.

"Wait, where'd my bed go? Why are we in a forest? WHY IS A WOMAN HOLDING MY ARM AND SNORING FOR CRYING OUT LOUD?" Ayron shrieked. He was shocked to find himself in the Forest and a princess, who was hugging his arm like a long-lost toy. Ekarto stood up on his feet but immediately collapsed on the spot, unfortunately finding out his legs were asleep. He screamed for help if anyone was there and a strange tribesman came crawling out of the green bushes, speaking a weird language. He howled and another person came rushing out, only walking this time.

"Sorry furr the delay, my daughter was eating a tree again," the tribesman said as if that was completely normal.

"Greetings, I'm—"

"Ah, I know who ya are already. Ya're Ekarto of Eldonville. Please, do follow us into the Queen's hut." Ayron snickered and laughed when he heard that the Queen lived in a hut.

"A bloody hut! Ha! Even the criminals in Eldonville get a house made of wood! Where do you all live in? BUSHES? Bahahaha! What inferior bums." The tribesman shot a nasty glance at him and simultaneously he moved some leaves out of the way, blocking their path. Behind all those leaves was a huge wooden palace.

The Forest Queen

The castle was impressive. It looked weak and fragile on the outside but on the inside, who knows what! The smell of wet leaves and flowers filled the air, with the sounds of birds and the screeches of monkeys surrounding the forests. The trees loomed over them, like frozen giants grounded into the earth forever. The ground was a semi-dry mud with specks of leaves, petals and pebbles littered and dispersed across the ground. The area around them had its own beauty. And of course, in the middle of it all, was the castle. It was a colossal fort with numerous flags and towers stationed at the top, with a great number of guards surrounding the area. Ekarto and the others walked into the palace and instead of walls made of logs and twigs, they found walls of brick and mortar. The actual castle was hidden beneath the wood, making this an impenetrable structure. This castle was meant to deceive the invaders! As they advanced, they found tapestries and paintings of the past like some coronations or wars. But then the tapestries on the walls ended, scratches and smudges ruining the ends.

"Why are the walls scratched? Was there a mistake in the paintings?" Zaula asked.

"No, no. It means there is nothing significant to paint. It leads right to the present day. Hm, tell you what, I think we should paint the Queen's marriage next. I hear she's looking for a husband." They continued to walk, gazing at everything inside the palace.

"So, you guys saw the dream?"

"What dream? I saw a vision of you speaking to some rocks that eventually turned into spirits, I think. Oh, and I also saw Okoto turn Eldonville into a huge workhouse place. Don't know what that was." Ekarto had also seen that vision. All the way back at Eldonville, Okoto was destroying homes, markets and farms to make way for workhouses and the peasants and middle-class citizens of the Eldonville Empire and Capital were forced to become workers, just like what happened back in the Conquest, when the nobles were fleeing to Silk City. Except this time it was on a larger scale. It's like they were preparing for some war.

As they walked down the hallway, a woman in vibrant green colours dashed out from a room out of the blue, a bag in her hand and wearing a little crown on her head. Her clothes were finely detailed and had gold and diamonds embroidered into her clothes. They looked very nice and comfy, yet heavy and tough to wear. She was almost slender, had a whole market of makeup on her face and wore many necklaces and bangles. To think the Forest Kingdom was poor. It was richer than Eldonville! She was probably the Forest Queen. An army of troops was marching towards her, all wearing dead animal skin and planks of wood for protection. Ayron thought they were pathetic and started making fun of them. It didn't go too well for him.

"Taarka, fetch me my royal dress! It's in my wardrobe. Corostar, go and get me my pet tiger. Badir is sleeping in my room. So, how can I help you people today?" Another man walked up to the Queen and saluted her.

"Glory to the Queen, ma'am."

"Thank you. So, where is this Ekarto person I was hearing about? Because there are a lot of men in my presence." Ekarto slowly walked towards the Forest Queen and she blushed at first sight.

"Greetings, Ekarto. My name is April. Queen April of the Forest Kingdom, 245th monarch of the Establishment of the Forest Kingdom Monarchy. How do you do?" Ekarto had mixed feelings. He felt scared, happy and confused, creating butterflies in his tummy.

"I'm, uh, fine?" The Queen was blushing even more, giggling a little and putting her mouth behind a fan she got out of her bag to show respect. She reached out her hand for Ekarto to shake and Ekarto shook it, not knowing how to feel. He had only ever met his uncle as king but never heard of the Forest Kingdom, nor did he ever meet a Queen in his life.

"So, what are we going to do now?" Zaula asked, her neck hurting from sleeping on a huge boulder.

"Oh, we go to this place with lots of walls and some shop called 'Enchanted Market'. Huh, it's a horrible name," Ekarto said. Leaftor, Zaula, Ayron and the other two were looking at Ekarto, confused. How did he know where to go and what to do next?

"Oh, you mean Harro," Queen April said. Now the confused faces were looking at the Queen and Ekarto, even more confused.

"Who's Harro?" The bandit asked.

"Harro isn't a person, you fool. It's a city near this one. Oh, if you wanted to know, this city is called Fortor. It's written on the walls. You'll see." She strutted away with confidence (and sass) and walked to her royal chamber, decorated with paintings, instruments, trophies, banners and royal artefacts to spice up the room. There was a massive bed with four posts holding up a fabric sheet, one that could roll down to make curtains. She got something from a chest and returned with a peculiar looking horn.

"You might want to cover your ears." Everyone present in the hall covered their ears and she sounded the horn that made a screechy and unpleasant sound. Some servants came and rang bells that tolled and rang mightily, creating a huge ruckus. The noises continued until they could see a shadow looming in from the other halls. It was a man. A strong, mighty man in front of them.

"I'm the Chief General. You can just call me Chief or Aburitsko or Chief Aburitsko if that sounds alright. Nice to meet you all." He held out his hand for everyone to shake and they reluctantly slipped their hands in his grasp.

Aburitsko was a tall and well-built brute. His face was almost built just for beards to grow. He had huge muscles, almost ripping from his clothes. He wore a turquoise cape, buttoned into his robes with gold buttons with green emblems encrusted into them, made from emeralds. He also wore many overalls and a belt that would go around his upper waist for some reason. He wore a helmet, supposedly an army one. His trousers were boringly plain but his shoes made up for it, curled and shiny with lots of detail. He was probably a very rich general to be wearing such attire.

"Well, it's indeed very nice to meet you all. Oh, I already said that."

He might have been a muscly man but his social skills were meagre. Weak, even. "Your Eminence, why did you ask to call me here? May I ask?" He politely said to April, bowing slightly.

"Oh, this fellow Ekarto, not that I *care* or anything, saw a vision of a shop in Harro. I think we need to go there, what do you say?"

"Well, this certainly calls for a journey to Harro. It'll only take an hour or so. So, Ekarto, is it? It's truly an honour to meet you. I know how much pain you must've gone through when you found out your father was killed. But with this opportunity and this amount of support, I think we have a window of success to destroy Okoto and re-establish peace and prosperity to Eldonville and the world." He also bowed slightly to Ekarto but was flicked on the ear by April.

"Well, Ekarto, what do you say to one who has just helped you with all of this?"

"Who?"

"Me! I accepted you into my territory, risking my kingdom and you can't even say a thank you to this fabulous queen right here! It is polite when a person bows." Ekarto was quite hesitant on this and Aburitsko started to make weird faces like he was kissing the air. Then he started to bow and kiss his own hands. He meant that Ekarto had to bow and kiss the hands of April, which was a weird custom to him. Nevertheless, he bowed like a gentleman and quickly kissed the hand of April, who started to giggle and blush more, almost fainting. Ekarto started to walk away with the rest of his little 'team', and April was giggling even more, skipping away and blushing. Who knows what she was thinking.

*****

"GLORY TO THE EMPEROR OF ELDONVILLE, PRAISE TO THE KING OF THE EMPIRE. I AM BLESSED TO BE IN THE PRESENCE OF YOUR GREAT MAJESTY, EMPEROR OKOTO, THE MAGNIFICENT. HAIL THE MASTER OF THE COUNTRY, I DO HOPE I AM NOT DISTURBING YOUR TIME," a watchman shouted as he came inside Okoto's room, who was writing on some sheets of paper and laughing under his breath.

"Come in, watchman. How are you?" Okoto asked, eyes glowing in the light of the sun.

"HOW CAN I BE FINER THA—"

"I'VE HEARD ENOUGH OF YOUR SCREAMS! Speak like a normal person. Inside voices. My ears cannot tolerate any shouting but mine and the hail you must speak. So, I ask again, HOW. ARE. YOU?" Okoto's veins started to turn purple and red, his teeth sharp and his mouth bloody again, his fingernails growing and his spine shooting bones out of his skin, his height growing. He stared right through the watchman, his eyes now bulging and red. The watchman was quivering and sweating. Okoto enjoyed the fear of his subjects.

"H-how can I b-be fin-finer than t-to meet y-you, your G-Great Highn-ness?" Okoto was calmer when he heard the response he should've heard and returned to a normal state again.

"So, what brings you here?"

"I have some terrible news, my king. Ekarto, his friend, Zaula and Leaftor aren't in Eldonville anymore. It seems they have disappeared or escaped." Okoto instantly became furious. He shouted in anger and knocked over his sheets of paper, holding a painting of Okarto and burning it.

"Looks like your son has escaped this time, brother. But his head will be at my feet! Aren't you happy to meet your son?" He cackled and sent the watchman away, who called for some ships to find Ekarto. Okoto looked again at the burning face of Okarto and spat on it, just as he did 23 years ago.

Journey to Harro

The orange sun slowly crept up into the horizon, sunshine bathing the forests and cities of the Forest Kingdom. Chickens and parrots squawked as the morning came. The Kingdom was becoming alive once more as the villagers and merchants woke from their slumber, welcoming the light of the sun. Back at the Forest Queen's palace, Ekarto and his team slept peacefully and quietly, unaware that it was time to wake up.

"WAKE UP EVERYONE! IT'S TIME TO EAT!" The residents in the palace woke up immediately and did their morning business to come down to the Royal Kitchen and grab their food. However, the little group that came yesterday were still sleeping until some guards came into their rooms with huge bells and gongs, sounding them with no care in the world. And it worked, obviously. They all woke up and were annoyed at the guards. But the guards had straight, long faces on. They showed no facial expressions and never would. They walked out of their rooms harmoniously like a little army of bell and gong sounders and marched to the Royal Kitchen to get their share of food too.

Ayron was the first of them all to go to the kitchen with the princess from who knows where and Zaula. They were attracted by the amazing smells of exotic and rich food they'd never tasted. The chefs served great portions onto their plates, and they all sat down and wolfed their food down. On the other hand, Ekarto, Leaftor and the bandit were not so hungry. They waddled their way to the Royal Kitchen, almost dropped their food but still had everything on their plates luckily and sat down to eat slower than paint drying. April was eating like a normal person and was amused to see how Ayron and the lot ate their food. Two completely different ways of eating food, yet one whole group altogether. Everyone in the Hall ate their food and gobbled it down, where it even got to a stage where they started licking their plates! The chefs were notoriously good at cooking and preparing food but this was beyond what they had seen their customers eat. They felt proud of themselves and went to a lobby to eat their own breakfast.

Every person in the hall rose from their chairs to get back to their days of long, hard work and making sure the Forest Kingdom was safe and stable. After all, Eldonville was nibbling away at Forest territory. Not that the Queen cared about the beaches of her country! Eldonville could have as much beach as they wanted. She was only worried about Harro and Fortor.

The servants cleared up after them and scurried off into the kitchens, scrubbing off the dirt. Queen April was escorted to the markets with some guards, where some fights were occurring. Aburitsko just stood there as if Ekarto had forgotten something they had to do.

"Um, is there something we have to do now?"

"Yes. We must leave immediately if we are to reach the ancient city of Vragos. We will ready ourselves to get to Harro and you, Ekarto, can do whatever that vision told you to do."

Ekarto, Aburitsko and the rest walked out of the border gates only to meet Queen April over there. Ayron kept telling Ekarto about a wart on his cheek, but he was ignored completely. Aburitsko bowed to April as she approached.

"Your Majesty, has the work been done in the marketplaces?"

"Yes. There was just an overpriced rotten coconut being sold. I arrested the merchant and he'll stand trial in the Royal Court at sunrise. What's happening now? Leaving so soon?" Queen April knew that they were already leaving for Harro and although this wasn't normal for any monarch in the Forest Kingdom, she wanted to tag along with them.

"General Xi, ready the palanquins. Multi sized. Also, ready my double palanquin. I will come too."

"But, Your Majesty! It is too risky for you to go! You could be robbed or killed or kidnapped!"

"If it is so risky for me, why are you sending Ekarto and everyone else there? Surely Ekarto needs to stay alive too! Ekarto is trying to save the whole world from disaster and you're all worried about my safety. At least care about the rest of us, will you? Tell the servants to get the palanquins set up. You may send troops if you feel it is necessary." General Xi's blood was boiling like a steaming cauldron of water inside him as he was April's uncle and mentor, yet April always decided to treat him in a bad way. He reluctantly bowed and stormed off to the servants to ready the Palanquins.

April led the group to the Royal Path, where the palanquins were surprisingly ready in just a few minutes apparently. Everyone got on, finding it very relaxing and comfortable. The seats were very soft, draped in a velvet sheet. It wasn't anything like a Forest Kingdom product. Normally, they'd be wooden or leafy.

"I like these palanquins! So beautiful…I think I'm going to vomit of happiness. Excuse me," Ayron said, rushing over to the nearest bush and spewing his meal.

Queen April climbed onto the seats, finding it difficult as her dress was huge and was too big for the entrance of the palanquin. After a few minutes of struggle, she finally was able to sit, her face turning red in embarrassment as she waited for everyone else to get on. Everyone else was able to sit comfortably and easily with no difficulty. Ekarto was the last to sit but he couldn't find a seat. Queen April smiled as she called Ekarto to her side, an empty seat beside her. *This is great!* Thought April. *I'm sitting with my true love!* Ekarto just smiled and waved nervously as April was drooling all over her dress, her eyes lost in his.

"Your Majesty, shall we be leaving now? We will be stopping shortly at the borders," a woman said. April was still under some sort of trance and Ekarto, not wanting to be rude, shook her shoulder to alert her.

"Uh, yes, we'll leave now. After we cross the borders, we shall collect some food, drink and relieve ourselves at the Haramara Station near Harro. Okay, now have we all got our passports?" At once, everyone started murmuring, passing weird looks at the Queen.

"What are passports?" The bandit asked. April's jaw dropped but was quickly closed in time by a servant as a fly was approaching her mouth. She slapped the servant's hand away and started laughing hysterically. Her feet kicked and kicked and she even kicked Ekarto's neck! When she calmed down, she wiped away a few tears and gasped for air.

"B-Basically, a p-pa-passport is something th-that you need to get around places. Without a p-passport people won't a-allow you to go anywhere in ca-case you are going to a city or country t-to do something against the law. I'm surprised that the Eldonvillians, grand masters of science, engineering and war don't know what passports are. They're just identification," she said, laughing in between. The bandit was offended. She did NOT come from Eldonville. Nor did the princess, but she didn't seem to care. Ekarto rolled his eyes at her childish behaviour and whispered something into her ears. April's eyes began to droop, her voice fading away and she rested her head on Ekarto's shoulder. Everyone started murmuring again and some were whistling excitedly.

"I used a drowsing chant on her. I took away her energy and stored it in my heart. Learned it back in the Silk Village from the clerics. After we reach the borders, I will restore half of her energy. The other half will be dissolved in case she starts acting up again." Ekarto explained. People looked horrified as if he had killed April. Ekarto rolled his eyes again. "I didn't kill her or take away all her energy. I just took most of it. She is fine. Don't worry." The servants of the Queen sighed in relief as they thought Ekarto had killed April to take over the Forest Kingdom. Looks like Ekarto wasn't here to conquer. *He just required help*, they thought. The lead horseman tapped and whistled to the horses and they started to trot gently, then galloping faster and faster until all you could see outside was a blur of green.

"Harro, here we come!" Zaula screamed.

Who's Who?

It had nearly been an hour but they hadn't reached Harro yet. Although the country was called the 'Forest Kingdom', this part of land was barren and dry, almost like a desert. They had crossed the borders and no one was there to protect the borders. It was just a long wall made from wood and had flags on top.

Everyone was bored and Ayron was the most bored of them all. But if you don't know what he's like so far, he likes fun. And even if there was a book to read, he'd call it fun.

Because he didn't know much of the people around here, nor did anyone know each other, Ayron tried to raise everyone's spirits by asking every single person there to speak about themselves.

"GUYS! I know this journey has been long and tiring but do not fear! For Ayron is here! Huh, eh?" Although he just started, it seemed he got a positive response. Everyone shuffled around in their correct sitting positions and listened to Ayron.

"People, people, people! We know ourselves, some of us know each other but other than that we are strangers to one another! So, in order for us to know each other a bit more, let's say a bit about ourselves! Your name, favourite thing to do, what you hate and a little backstory! Starting with this woman over here! So, what is your name?" Ayron pointed at the bandit, who was slumped in her seat. The bandit looked quite uncomfortable but with a smile and re-assurance from Ayron, she felt more confident and spoke.

"Hi, my name is Hina. Um, I am 21 years old and I like to run and do lots of exercise. I hate public speaking but nowadays I am coming over it. A bit about me is that I come from a country called Boryinvi, up north near the Tao Mainlands and east from the Imperial Fire Tribes. A little bit more about me is that I wasn't gifted with any powers, so I rely on my fighting and running skills to survive. I have absolutely no idea why I came here! One minute I was robbing some people and the next I am sleeping on a stone slab in the Forest Kingdom! Well, the only thing left for me to say is that my father was killed by some Eldonvillian archers and they tortured him in front of my eyes. Maybe that's why I was destined to destroy the Empire with you guys." She was quite red from embarrassment but people clapped and showed their sympathy to her father's loss as it seemed. Ayron then started to survey who to pick next and out of nowhere he picked the mysterious princess from who knows where.

"Hello! My name is Mia and I am the princess of a kingdom in the country of Cabourice. My kingdom's name is Modantis, however, I'm not the heir to the throne. My older sister is the heir, whose name is Felicity. I like to sleep and learn anything I can. I hate eating coconuts because they have a weird texture and they taste, well, tasteless. I kind of already said a bit about me but something else I can say is that my favourite animal is a bear." She growled at Ayron and he did it back. He was in awe of Mia's story and then thought of who to think of who to pick next. Out of the blue, he heard a weird groaning and a bit of laughter. And it seemed impossible but April was awake! Ekarto, like all the others, were beyond shocked.

"Hehe, I was awake for a few minutes. Nice to know you guys a bit more. And it's about time that the star of this whatever you call it, me, starts to tell you all a bit about myself."

"Wait, but I was going to pick Leaf—"

"LADIES FIRST, AYROONIE!"

"Ayroonie? That's a horrible nickname for me." But April shoved his face away, causing the palanquin to jolt a bit. She brushed off some imaginary dust from her shoulders and then she cleared her throat to speak.

"Greetings! It is I, Queen April! Otherwise known as Eika April Taolung. I absolutely adore my crowns and my nation. I hate people wasting my time, which is extremely irrelevant. It's like people don't understand that YOU HAVE A LIFE TO LIVE! A little bit more about me is that I have a direct bloodline link to the infamous Barghtan VI, the greatest yet cruellest conqueror of the world in prehistoric times! Basically, before much of the nation was formed! His empire conquered much of the world but he died before the world was fully conquered and became his territory, so his daughter Sadira II of Pakotisbania ruled the Empire for a long time!" Everyone was quite interested in her story, but Ekarto wasn't. Either he just didn't like April or he thought his story was far more impressive. No one could tell. Ayron then, just like he planned to, picked Leaftor as he knew nothing of him.

"Me? I'm quite a boring person. I'd kill everyone here of boredom!" Leaftor pleaded with Ayron to skip him but Ayron as usual was stubborn.

"Come on, Leaftor! At least we'll know what you're like! Tell you what, I'll give you time to say your whole life story. Go on then, Leaftor! Even if I die here because of how boring you are, I'll be glad knowing who you were. Huh, people?" There was a tired cheering going on but it was sufficient for Leaftor to say his story which indeed isn't boring (Or maybe it is.)

"My name is Tinror Maguran, otherwise known as Leaftor. I never knew my parents as they left me in an Eldonvillian city called Arsotros, not too far from Eldon's City. They left me all alone, possibly to leave me to die there. I'll never know. But I was brought up in a fort where some priests called me Leaftor and I named myself Tinror. Everyone had a last name there as Maguran, so I accepted it as my own last name. I had a good life of patience and prosperity but it all changed when I was 15. At that age, there were some Fire Bandits who raided the little fort where I lived and they massacred everyone there. They left me out because I looked foreign and they thought I was held captive there, so they freed me from their prisons. I sought refuge in the Eldonville Palace, where I was caught by Ekarto's grandfather stealing food from his pantry, which was obviously a big crime. He let me go and even though his best advisor insisted I should be killed. He made me a minister in the palace and I became Okarto's very good friend who was 7 at the time. My story pretty much ends there. But then it begins again when Okoto bathed me in boiling water when I was told secret information about Okarto's death no one knew about. No one knew Okarto was killed by Okoto! He also arrested the witness of the murder." Unlike the other stories, this seemed to be the most intriguing one yet! They clapped and whistled and celebrated and Leaftor felt in ways he couldn't express. Ayron started to count who said their part and who didn't and he was left with him and Ekarto.

"Well, since I began this thing we're doing and you know what they say, best for last, I think we should hand it over to Ekarto! Wooh!" Just as usual they clapped so that Ekarto could say who he was. But this time April cheered the most and encouraged others to cheer for him. Even Zaula encouraged the others!

"Well, hello then. My name is Ekarto, you'll probably know and I am the heir to the Eldonville throne. I like playing this board game called Gargwon, where you and your opponent have 50 pieces together to make an army and the first to take over the centrepiece or the tower as I know it wins the game. I don't like eating fish because of the bones and it makes me sick. Something you probably don't know about me is that I was once hit on my head with a plank with a nail because people thought I was an Eldonvillian spy. I wasn't and Ayron was the one that healed and treated me." Ayron smiled and bowed and both April and Zaula looked engaged in Ekarto's story.

"Tell us more!" Zaula pleaded with Ekarto and April did so too. Ekarto decided not to raise any argument or make things bad, so he went on about his past life in Silk Village before he came to Eldonville.

"Um, okay. Another thing is that me and Ayron used to play Gargwon so much that we invented our own championships for it. We even invented more pieces, games and were one day confiscated from the game for a week. We just played Gargwon on the sand, where we carved out the grid and pieces with rocks and twigs. Maybe we could play again, Ayron." Ayron looked excited to play Gargwon again with Ekarto and now it was his turn to speak. He bowed and cleared his throat, trying to amuse the passengers on board but it was worthless. He went straight to the point and started, "Yes. It is I. The one. And only. Friend. Of Ekarto. I. am. AYRON."

"HURRY UP ALREADY," Hina screamed.

"All right. Cool down. Anyways, my name is Tihn Ayron Gepha III, son of Tinyan Goronan Gepha and Mirdis Fauriya Gepha and I come from the Silk Village, although my family comes from the Air Provinces. I like Gargwon, just like Ekarto, and absolutely LOATHE trolls. Something you don't know about me is that when I was born, my mother was going to call me Cafdan but my grandmother changed it to Ayron. Now I realise how grateful I should be that my name isn't Cafdan. It sounds horrendous." He received a few claps from Princess Mia and Ekarto and some whistles from Hina and Leaftor and Zaula. He was saddened to see he got some of the worst reactions.

"How long until we get to the Haramara Station? I need food." Ayron was groaning and looked ill. However, he instantly became excited when he saw walls and towers far away in the distance.

"HARRO! WE'RE HERE!"

"Did we really just miss Haramara? I was looking forward to eating again," Hina said.

The Duke of Harro

The palanquins came to a halt and there were some soldiers who rushed to them and opened the doors of the palanquins. Queen April stepped out of the palanquin, her dress flowing out like a body of water flowing onto the dead seabed. Ekarto helped her out and opened the doors for his friends. He also paid the soldiers and guards and horsemen for helping them get across but they refused the Eldonvillian currency. They started to travel back to their home in the Capital and Ekarto and his friends were left there. They turned around to face the city of Harro and they were amazed to see what was in front of them.

There were walls that stretched throughout the whole city, farther than the eye could see. There were also inscriptions and logos on the walls that looked old and were smudged. Banners of the Harro City Insignia were draped onto the walls to make it look more presentable. They could hear a lot of noise and chatter behind the walls, so Ayron, being the most excited of them all, led everyone inside, where it was livelier and more fun than the outside landscape, a dry desert with almost little to no life.

People were dressed very modestly and had expensive looking clothes on. They walked and talked and did their own daily business, like buying produce from the markets or going to work. There was a robust and ginormous bazaar in front with many people buying and selling and trading and supplying. Patrols and Guards walked around the perimeter of the walls, surveying the area to make sure the city was all safe and well. They could also see tall towers and houses in the far distance. It seemed that the whole city was divided into different parts. Flags kept flapping in the wind and there was a tall statue of a man wearing expensive clothes and a pointy hat, possibly a crown. He was smiling and there was a huge flag of the Harro Insignia flapping behind him.

"Who's that?" Leaftor asked.

"Oh, that's my cousin, Katan the Sixth. He rules Harro, son of my dad's sister. Of course, I don't have that many cousins to rule the whole Forest Kingdom but just the important cities are ruled by my cousins and siblings. Katan is one of them and although he is quite crazy and weird, he has managed to keep Harro stable." She looked around the city and was quite impressed to see that Harro had seriously been improved far greater than its previous duke had ever did, Duke Farginan I, his father. Harro had been under a state of civil war for many years and Katan looked like he was able to fix the economy and building crises and re-establish the city to make it as powerful as ever. Although it was Queen April who stopped the war back when she was only 19, it was Katan the Sixth who constructed Harro to be the best city it could possibly be. The walls couldn't be fixed but what was beneath the walls could be fixed and all of it already was fixed.

Everyone dispersed to explore their own parts of Harro. Hina went with Zaula to the markets. Ayron went around the streets and great attractions in the city. Leaftor was chatting with some builders talking about his own nonsense, and April and Mia were chatting about their families and their royalty. Ekarto was just stranded near the entrance of the Harro Wall. Then he felt someone tapping him.

"Ayron, you can stop bugging me about your wart."

"Who's Ayron? What wart are you talking about? Who am I? Or you? This world is crazy." Ekarto turned back to see it wasn't Ayron and his wart but a rather peculiar teenager with very elaborate clothes and a pointy hat. Then it dawned on Ekarto that THIS teenager was probably the Duke, as the statue also had a pointy hat and had quite similar faces. Ekarto didn't know how to feel meeting the Duke, but he felt it was no big deal. Just a Duke.

"Oh, for the love of Pakota, I forgot to introduce myself! I am Duke Katan, the Sixth. I am Harro's GREATEST duke and possibly the greatest duke of Harro! Did I say that twice? I think I said that twice. Oh, I forgot you were there, ha-ha. Who are you exactly?"

The Duke seemed like quite a feisty and playful person but that wasn't what Ekarto was thinking about. Looking at the rest of the citizens of Harro, he answered back to Katan, "You have a very nice city to rule. Nice people, nice materials, nice structures. You're a lucky Duke," Ekarto said, his voice gentle and calm as if he was being hypnotised.

"Hmm, you could do with shortening your name, huh? Your name is like, uh, three sentences long! C'mon, surely that's not your name!"

"My name is Ekarto. I'm Okoto's nephew."

"Sweet Leaves of my mother, the enemy is here! Sound the alarms! Run for your lives and panic like there's no tomorrow! Throw yourself in the rivers because why not! Cry and scream because who knows if today is your last day! He's going to burn us with his fiery wrath and his sorcery! Harro is doomed! Mother, save me—" Ekarto shook Katan quite violently, resulting into him twirling around and bumping into one of the construction towers. The construction tower was made simply from twigs and vines roped up together, so it was very fragile. It toppled over but Leaftor caught it just in time with some roots he grew from the ground. The builders inside clung onto the rails and bars, fearful that this day would be their last. Once the tower was positioned and fastened with some other roots torn from under the soils of Harro, the builders speedily climbed down the tower and thanked Leaftor for saving them. Katan still felt dizzy when he came back to Ekarto and still was scared of Ekarto. Zaula saw the incident and ran over to Katan.

"What's happening here?"

"The Duke think's I'm the enemy. Zaula, care to explain?"

"Katan, Ekarto isn't the enemy. In fact, he is trying to end the enemy. The Emperor of Eldonville killed Ekarto's father who was supposed to become King. Now Ekarto must avenge his death. Please, can you understand?" Katan 'shook' his fear away and reached out his hand to shake Ekarto's but coiled his legs back in fear. Ekarto shook it and went away, getting other visions of the shop in Harro. He started to go towards it, using some signs to indicate where the shop was. Katan ran away from Ekarto and ran inside his mansion.

The Magic Shop

Ekarto started to walk deeper into the City Centre of Harro, where numerous markets and houses lined up a massive street. Some of the shops sold different types of leaves, trees and soil for people in Harro to use for their own needs. Other shops sold magical items like wands and animals that could speak. Of course, these animals were deadly. At least three shops sold weapons for the army and armour for them too. The other shops sold food, clothes, drinks and their own services. But one shop caught Ekarto's eye. It was the very shop he saw in his vision. The 'Enchanted Market' was in front of him, looking older and more run-down than the other shops. It had broken planks supporting the main structure and a hanging sign with the paint coming off. He went inside, where a few bells rang as he came in. Inside, there were an array of shelves stacked with stones with labels describing their properties.

There were green stones that had labels of healing and nurturing properties, blue ones that had labels of water and freezing properties and natural disasters associated with wind and cloud. There were grey stones that had labels of strength and metal and beige stones with labels of Earth and wealth and earthquakes. There were purple stones with labels of magic and poison and there were red stones with labels of fire, lava, volcanoes, destruction, warmth, anger, demons and the sun. These were stones that could aid Ekarto in his battle with Okoto but should he take them from this shop? Firstly, the stones were too expensive in Harroan currency, 50,000 Lyri coins for each stone. And the purple, red and blue stones were an additional 13,000 Lyri coins, with needs for a license, which costs 200,000 Lyri for admission and an advance of 1,000 Lyri for tax. Secondly, the old woman at the store was not the one you could probably trust. She looked like a witch and always seemed to stare awkwardly at people who passed by, and her shop was different from all the others, isolated but looks didn't matter. Ekarto knew never to judge a person by their face. So, he went over to the shopkeeper, who was brushing her nails against a table and chewing her frizzy, blue hair (Yes. She has blue hair.)

"Welcome to Shama's Enchanted Market store, where we sell all magical items available to the world. How can I help you?" She said, no expression in her voice at all.

"I just came to look around, that's all," Ekarto uttered with a nervous laugh slapped into his sentence.

"Oh, that's what they all say, chump. But I'll give ya some news, Son. No one leaves without an item from my shop. What makes you so special?" she stated, threats trailing in her voice.

"I've got no money."

"You? No money? Sonny, ya body is made of money! Look at it, gold chains and silk fabrics and other expensive fabrics line ya up! And ya say ya got no money? Tch, tch, tch. Ya shouldn't spend on clothes before making a business. That's what I told my son." Ekarto didn't know what the woman was talking about but when he saw his clothes in the mirror, he was astonished. Beautiful fabrics went around his waist, his trousers made from gold silks and jewels fused into his long necklace, rubies crested onto each little chain. There was a carving of the Eldonville crest on his chain medal with a picture of his mother on it. She was beautiful, a warm smile comforting him. He had a green sword strapped to his back and a gold tie on his bun with two red strings floating in the air. He looked like a king and somehow he didn't notice it this whole time. Once he just started to check out his shoes made from Bull leather, the shopkeeper started to tap her long nails on the table violently.

"Um, excuse me. This ain't some clothes store. Either you buy, donate or get out of my house." Ekarto was startled by her and started to look around the shelves. Stones, wands, hats, bottles of spells, books, eyestones, telescopes and robes.

"Um, is there anything else other than what's here?" Ekarto asked.

"Yeah. There are ancient cards from the Kanagur Era, some brooms, amulets, elixirs, medals, splinters from the Great Wizard's Branch, staves, summoning hoods and eye covers." Ekarto seemed to be uninterested in the items but three of the items caught his attention. Staves, hoods and eye covers. The very items Okoto has. Ekarto thought that Okoto must've bought them from somewhere and maybe this shop was one of them. Yes, it was a rickety, old building and the shortest of them all but Ekarto felt like he was somehow attached to this shop in many ways. He couldn't explain it but he knew it.

He mustered the courage to go up to the shopkeeper, who was chewing some chilli nuts and asked the very question that could possibly determine his success or failure against Okoto…

"DO YOU KNOW A MAN THAT COULD'VE COME TO THIS SHOP?" He shrieked, his words spitting from his mouth like greased lightning.

"Son, ya ask some stupid questions. Any man could've waddled in here and bought something from here. If you're asking for some particular fellow, describe him or give me his name. All customers give their name. Not you, of course. You're mental." Ekarto felt quite hurt at her remark but it was best not to reveal his identity now. Who knows what this witch of a woman could do once she found out.

"He looks quite royal, mad, sharp teeth, tall, broad, a heavy voice and a crown?"

"Sweet tap-dancing monkeys you just described yaself except for the sharp teeth and crown. You aint got any of those." Ekarto thought long and hard about Okoto. He only met him for a few days, so he didn't know much about him. Maybe his talking style? No, too revealing. His identity? No, too suspicious. Saying that he's a murderer? No, too vague. Then it hit him. In one of those weird spiritual dreams, there was a vision of him wearing his eye covering and a detailed look at his staff. A long, dark staff with feathers of exotic birds, special stones, skulls, enchanting splinters, cards and one, big, red gemstone on the top. All of those items circled the staff, covering it completely except for a little bit of fabric for the grip. It had a huge skull of a frog on the top with three skulls of some baby turtles circling the bigger skull. There was a long, blue spear at the end of the stick, so Okoto could stick the staff into any floor he wished. There were strange carvings on it and whenever he did a spell, they would glow red. Okoto's eye cover was red and transparent. Although his eyes were naturally brown, he put on his eye cover to make his left eye look red. His right eye was apparently just red. Ekarto exclaimed when he saw his staff. So much, the shopkeeper was startled.

"Whatchya fussing about, son?"

"This customer. Did he buy a long, dark staff with some frog skulls and exotic feathers? With a blue spear at the end?" Ekarto bellowed.

"Um, let me have a yeep bit of a think." She thought hard but not long. She kept drumming her nails on her counter (seems to be her thing) and then her eyes lit up.

"Yes! There is a customer! Some strange fellow said his name was Yeroa. Comes from the outskirts of the Arctic Ring of the Water Kingdom. Had a big woolly coat, pet seal and a bone spear. He also bought some eye covers."

Ekarto was so happy, he couldn't hold it. He started to shake the shop with happiness and ran around, flailing his arms everywhere. The woman in the shop had to put him in a trance, make him pay 20 Gindars (Gindars is Eldonvillian currency) for breaking a staff and an additional three Gindars for a magical map. She threw him out in immense fury and shut her door with a powerful slam, showing a 'CLOSED FOR NOW YA MORONS' sign. Ekarto still was excited and ran to the Harro border station, where his friends were still 'camping' in. Ayron and Princess Mia were cuddling and staring at the sun, Leaftor was eating some tomatoes, Hina was trying to steal some gold from a Harro citizen, until Zaula stopped her and Queen April was chatting with the Admiral of the Harro Assassins about strategies to protect Harro from raiders.

Kidnapped

Ekarto ran towards them and jumped in excitement, unable to contain his eagerness anymore.

"GUYS! I FOUND OUT SOMETHING! OKOTO GOES TO THIS SHOP I JUST WENT TO, THE ENCHANTED MARKET!" He was desperate to see the reactions of his friends but no one was happy. In fact, they seemed confused about what he was talking about.

"Ekarto, how is this relevant? You're not powerful enough to fight him. Anyways, he doesn't buy his items from anywhere. Rather, he just makes them himself. Did the shopkeeper find out who you are or did she know Okoto?" Ekarto's smile gradually turned into a frown. He was so excited when finding out but he didn't realise that it was useless. So what if Okoto did or didn't go there? Stupid! He became all sad and also realised they had to come to Harro for no reason whatsoever.

"Well, Ekarto seems to have got some new clothes. Were they for a bargain or what?" April noticed that he looked like a King, just like he noticed himself. Everyone was amazed to see his outfit, especially Ayron and April.

"You look like you can afford the whole world! I didn't know you could find clothes like this here," Hina said.

"You look so nice in this! Wait, who's that woman on your medal? Gosh, IS THAT YOUR WIFE? WHY DIDN'T YOU TELL ME YOU'RE MARRIED?" April shouted.

"That's not my wife, I don't even have one. It's my mother, Okinara. She was imprisoned with Leaftor in Eldonville."

"THEN HOW DOES YOUR MOTHER LOOK YOUNGER THAN YOU?"

"I don't know! I didn't pick this, it just came like that, like magic." Then Ekarto explained that he didn't buy this or have it made. In fact, it came by itself. He cooled down with April and they then decided what to do next. But it was solved for them when a little bird flew and clung onto Ekarto's arm and had a note in its beak. He read it, saying that it was a message from Aburitsko.

"Once you're done with Harro, walk to the city of Davalgor and catch a boat to the Fire Tribes. You'll reach there within a week or so. There should be plenty of food and necessities on the boat ready for you all, just be patient. Good day, Chief General Aburitsko of the Forest Kingdom, 2nd Order of the Inferior Knights."

They were quite worried when Aburitsko said 'walk' to Davalgor but April wasn't fazed by this at all.

"Davalgor is actually right next to this city. Just a few minutes of walking and we'll be there. It's a Sea City. We'll get a boat from the harbour, then we sail to the coast of the Fire Tribes. All that clear to you?" They all nodded, carried all their souvenirs and shopping and walked outside of Harro to Davalgor City. Katan could be heard from the distance screaming:

"BYE, APRIL. COME AGAIN SOON. BYE, LEAFTOR. THANKS FOR SAVING THE BUILDERS. BYE, AYRON. YOU'RE WEIRD. BYE-"

But they continued to walk and tried to muffle him out. And eventually they did, seeing the tall posts of Davalgor nearby.

Davalgor was a weird city. It was built on some wooden logs and posts to make sure the tide wouldn't flood the city. It had a wooden floor and the citizens had to live in these small houses that were built on the top of the platform. It was a good idea but then the other half of the city was normal, built on the natural terrain of the Forest Kingdom, not some posts and platforms. April explained that this was not so much of a major city, so it wasn't ruled by a family relative of hers but a robust and lively mayoress. Ekarto saw that there was a shortcut to the harbour, which was simply a curved path to the area instead of going through the actual city and maybe slowing down due to how many people lived there. When they reached the harbour, they saw some boats but there was one boat that April wanted to go on, and this was the Queen's Boat.

Queen April, let me tell you, had thousands of things. 500 dresses, 20 pets, 100 forts, 300 castles, 50 fans, 403 bags, 60 crowns and 125 ships all belonging to her. There were many more but what was important was that she owned 125 boats. One boat for each city. They were all different as they had to look more 'adapted' to what the city was like. If it was swampy it'd be a green, leafy boat. If it was a sea city, like Davalgor, it'd be blue and it'd have resemblances of the sea, like fish and coral painted onto the boat. This very one in front of them was a majestic one, with a mermaid at the end pointing to the sun. It had hundreds of golden chains strapping and tying the sails. Rope ladders were tied tightly into the masts and floorboards, making it sturdy and easy for the sailors to climb on. There were great flags on top of the posts and there were lots of crossbows and other weapons on the ship to protect them. Beside it was a smaller ship with around 50 soldiers, five boulders on each side and three crossbows on each side. The Queen really needed a lot of protection.

April started to climb onto the ship with everyone else but then something bad happened. The 'soldiers' present were starting to rush towards everyone and knock them out. After that, they were dragged away.

"Open your eyes." Ekarto was feeling a lot of pain on his head when he woke up from his temporary concussion and when he did, he was petrified to see who was in front of him. It was a woman and some group of grim-looking men who were wearing masks on their faces to hide their identities and holding spears and shields made from simple wooden planks and rock blades tied onto the stick with some ropes. The woman waved her hand violently in front of Ekarto's face and he reacted to let her know he was awake.

"Good. You're awake. So, tell me. Do you know what your father has done?" He was confused. They went through all this to ask him that? Well, he didn't know what Okarto had done. So, he gave an example of how he boosted the economy of Silk Village and turned it into Silk City!

"LIES! ALL LIES! Okoto is ruining the whole world! And you better stop it! I am holding you ransom until Okoto pays for your return and ends this empire. Your friends will burn if you don't tell me what Okoto's planning next." Now Ekarto understood what was happening. They mistook Ekarto for Okoto's son! That is, if he had any.

"No, wait, I'm not Okoto's son, I'm Ekarto. Son of Okarto." They went silent and then laughed hysterically, spitting on his face slightly.

"YOU? SON OF OKARTO? THAT'S LIKE TELLING ME THAT I AM THE DAUGHTER OF THE MOON! HAHAHAHA! Oops." Ekarto smirked at them. He now knew who these people were, just by their choice of words. They were people of the Moon Clan.

"No, seriously, I'm Ekarto." Their laughter did reduce a bit but they were still not believing him.

"I know. Maybe we could look into your eyes," one of the men said. The woman in front of Ekarto liked that idea, so she looked deeply and carefully at Ekarto's eyes. She gasped and was astonished by what she could see.

Okarto had brown eyes that had bluish and purple pigments waves around his pupil that needed to be looked into carefully. They were aligned in a way like waves of colours around Okarto's iris. Surely the son had the same eyes? Yes, the son should've and Ekarto did except he had another colour, red. The rebels would have known what Okarto's eyes would look like through constant visions. Ekarto had the same eyes as Okarto, same face as Okarto, body similarly built like Okarto and Okinara and a personality of his ancestors, all mixed in together. How could they not realise Ekarto had the same face as Okarto, just a bit different? Maybe his eye positioning and nose looked different and more like Okinara but everything else was the same. The woman stepped back in awe when she realised Ekarto truly was Okarto's son and bowed in honour.

"I don't want you to bow. I'm not that special, you know." But she continued to bow and ordered the men behind her to release Ekarto's friends and let them go wherever they had to.

"So, Ekarto, how do you want to defeat Okoto? You can tell us and we'll tell this to the other nations of the world. Maybe even the Tao Dynasty might pitch in to help!" The Tao Dynasty, if you didn't already know, was a mighty empire that was taking over their neighbouring countries and hoping to create an empire for the wealth and prosperity of the Emperor. It was bigger and stronger than Eldonville's younger Empire. And a lot older. If they rallied a war against the Eldonvillians, they would win but they didn't want to go to war with them until they started to attack colonies belonging to the Tao Emperor. If Ekarto could just persuade them to help him, maybe they'd give support to his army. But this was just the beginning, and they didn't even finish their main task in Vragos: to release the spirits.

"I was thinking we could make a huge army made up of other soldiers across the world and defeat Okoto in a war." The kidnappers liked the sound of this, and even offered their service to escort them to the Fire Tribes to release the spirits from their stones and some soldiers to add to their army. Their army had just grown by 20!

Ekarto thanked the kidnappers for their services and left with his friends to the shores to find that they had been on the shores of Davalgor the whole time. The Queen's ship was still there, so they hurriedly ran to it and went on deck, the soldier ships and moon clan soldiers escorting them to the Fire Tribes. One week of travelling on the sea, and it was going to go smoothly.

Hopefully.

The Fleet Battle

It had been almost four days of travelling. It was quite peaceful, but there was nothing to do. They all tried playing Gargwon altogether but gave up when Ayron kept winning. When Leaftor joined the game, he demolished Ayron. They also tried to do fishing but there was nothing to fish with. All they could do was eat, sleep and stare into the empty sea. The soldiers on the other boats were always on the lookout and always moved their crossbows and their fire projectors to aim for any suspicious ships. Many of the vessels they passed by were not trying to fight the Queen's Fleet but they were only traders and fishing boats and the soldiers weren't too worried until the last day when they could see land. There were some other boats patrolling the land but they weren't from the Fire tribes. To their horror, they were Eldonvillian boats. The Guzreed-Indeli Navy.

The small fleet of five, named the Guzreed-Indeli Navy, was a selected group of pirates and soldiers who worked together for Emperor Okoto and their Sea Generals. They had lightweight wooden boats but there were higher ranked boats in the same navy. These boats that the Queen's Fleet was facing were of the highest rank, Guzreed-Indeli Victory Boats. Although they were still made from wooden planks and tied up loosely, they were also reinforced with metal and had revolutionary weapons stationed to protect them and there were five Victory boats that had just noticed the incoming Queen's fleet, so they slowly turned towards them and started firing arrows and rocks and boulders catapulted from the deck. The soldiers from the Queen's fleet started to smash ginormous boulders onto the hulls of the Guzreed-Indeli boats, causing their decks to break and sinking the boats. They kept doing so and Zaula kept making waves at the opposing force to twist the boats and make them confused but the waves were sliced in half by the boats' sharp blades at the front of the boats. The battle went on for an hour.

It was almost sundown and they continued to fight. The Queen's soldiers were now using their fire projectors to burn the nearing Victory ships and the warriors and pirates on the other side were continuously firing boulders and arrows at the Queen's Ship, Ekarto and his friends trying to avoid the arrows. Then Ekarto became angry and started to throw flames at the Guzreed-Indelies (he's impatient, you know). They were coiling back in fear but they continued aiming their arrows at Ekarto, who successfully created a barrage to burn away all the projectiles fired at him and mercilessly burning the ships trying to attack the Queen's Fleet. He even saw some soldiers sailing towards the Moon Clan soldiers and fighting them, so he went over to them and injured them severely with his fire until they retreated to their own boats. The Guzreed Captain, Indeli Admiral and Eldonvillian Corporal decided to turn back and all that was left was a packed Guzreed-Indeli boat with more than 400 soldiers and pirates sailing away to Eldonville slower than a turtle floating in the sea. Ekarto was relieved when he successfully fended off the enemy and the soldiers cheered and hugged. April hugged Ekarto and Zaula excitedly squeezed Ekarto. They were extremely happy of their victory in their first battle with the Eldonvillians and it was even better when they realised they had just reached the coastal Imperial Fire Tribe village that was welcoming them. The Kuyterc Village.

Battle of Kuyterc

They arrived peacefully on the shores of the Fire Tribes, where they were welcomed and cheered for by some villagers. They arrived at a village called 'Kuyterc'. There were some Village leaders dressed in unique clothes and robes made from old cotton. They held staffs with phoenixes and flames on the staff to symbolise they have the power of fire. They were quite old and stern-looking but inside they were friendly folk who just wanted to see who came to their tribe and when they did, they were astounded to see Ekarto. They scurried to him as quickly as they could and leaned their staff towards Ekarto's head and his friends' heads as a sign of greeting and blessing.

"Welcome to the Kuyterc Village in the Kuytercan sector. Never have I been more pleased to see you, Ekarto. Your ancestors have roots deep down to this nation and we're glad you're here. We're absolutely sorry about your father's death, it was indeed brutal." Ekarto felt a warming sensation in his heart as if he arrived home and was welcomed by his parents or grandparents. Out of nowhere, he hugged all of the leaders and they hugged him back, claiming Okarto had done this too when Ukarto was dying of his disease.

"Let me introduce you to ourselves. My name is Kerda and I am 83 years old. His name is Kartu, very close to your name and he is my younger brother who is 75 years old. My elder sister's name is Akoia, who is 90 years old and my other younger brother, Zorok, who is 80 years old. I like to think of you all as my little grandchildren because my own are far away into the Central City sorting out the Eldonville and Tao Crisis. We want you to feel like you're at home and to you, Ekarto, this country is your home as well as Eldonville. Enjoy!" The leaders walked away, chatting excitedly of Ekarto's arrival.

"Okarto truly has given a unique son to this world."

"I agree but will he be able to defeat Okoto?"

"Yes. With his kind of power, he can defeat the whole world single-handedly. He just hasn't learnt his skill yet."

"I'm hungry."

The next day, Ekarto woke up excitedly with Ayron and Hina when they smelt the food coming from the village house, where everyone would gather to eat their food and spend time together if they wished to. Once the hungry trio entered the house, they saw dishes and plates full of piping hot and steaming dishes with sides of many exotic fruits and dessert. There were huge cauldrons and bowls of chicken and cow and sauces mixed with them, coming with rice and rolls of vegetables and radishes and spring onions served with slight scorches on the sides to make it dry and crispy, just like Ekarto liked it. There were also many fruits like apples and pineapples and mangoes mixed together to make the form of a castle, a salad made to look majestic. They sat down, greeted the incoming guests for breakfast and ate very modestly but in large amounts too. The rest of Ekarto's friends, Leaftor,

Mia, Zaula and April came late to the breakfast as they wanted to sleep more and they ate as if all energy was drained from them but you couldn't argue, they had gone through a lot.

Once breakfast was over, April decided to go out and sunbathe whilst Ayron, Hina, Leaftor and Zaula were going to play with the children of the village. Mia thought of joining April as they were both royalty, so she did. Ekarto was talking about his experiences in the past few days with the leaders whilst they talked about their memories of Ekarto's parents and grandparents and the eldest, Akoia, even meeting his great-grandmother Ikarta the Great, who was 15 when she first met Akoia, who was only five years old. They were good friends, and Ekarto's great grandmother funded the Kuyterc Village when they went under lots of debt and taxes. All was going well for them, and it seemed like they had found peace.

They weren't sure about it, though.

Okoto paced around his room, awaiting his missing fleet of Guzreed-Indeli soldiers. They were expected to come the day before but unfortunately they were apparently caught in a storm so they were delayed by a day, and it was taking hours for them to arrive. Okoto was about to announce them dead to their families and friends but then they were seen in the docks near the palace, unharmed but in very tight spaces. Only one boat arrived and this was what worried Okoto even more. Were his men okay? Did any of them drown? Were they all ill? He rushed over to them and met the 400 soldiers he sent.

"Thank the stars for returning you all in one piece. I see no one was lost to the storm." They looked ashamed and disappointed and they then blurted out it wasn't a storm but it was Ekarto and some other boats burning them and trying to kill them.

"WHAT? You found Ekarto? And you LOST to him? Did he have any soldiers with him or what?" They nodded and said there were 50 or so soldiers who were extremely skilled from the Forest Kingdom. Although Okoto was angry at Ekarto, he was still thankful they returned in one piece, all safe and sound. He then remembered that they saw where Ekarto was heading. The soldiers were stationed at the Imperial Fire Tribes, so he must've been heading there. Okoto smiled cunningly when he realised this and ordered for his defeated men to rest and recover while an army would sail to the Fire Tribes to raid them and capture Ekarto once and for all. It was a massive army and indeed this was too much for the Kuyterci People to handle.

A skilled group of 5000 samurai, 25 siege weapons and 25 ships were sent to the Fire Tribes with 200 samurai and one siege weapon on one boat. Truly, this was a fierce battle waiting to happen. Okoto splashed some potions and spells onto the boats to make them go to the Tribes faster than a Groccon Eagle, which was the fastest bird in the world, able to fly to the Tribes in just three hours. The ships would go in under two hours. Now, the war was coming to the Kuytercs.

April and Mia were now stretching and tanning in the sun but their skin had barely tanned. Ekarto was STILL talking with the leaders but this time about how to perfect his power of fire. Leaftor was admiring the sea view as he had nothing better to do. Ayron, Hina and Zaula were playing with the children.

A fisherman was inside the village house and was talking to a friend of his, probably about fish. They spoke in a foreign language that Ekarto had never heard of before. Maybe this was the native language in the Kuyterc Village? He was deep into his conversation, but stopped dead in his tracks when he saw something out of the window. His friend asked why he suddenly stopped talking, and when he looked outside, he looked terrified. The fisherman screamed something twice in his language, causing unrest. The leaders heard the language and Ekarto heard too, but he didn't understand it. He went outside to see why there was so much commotion and then he saw what he wished was a nightmare. A whole fleet of ships coming towards Ekarto, packed with samurai. The leaders and warriors from the village made up a small army of 200 against a 5,000 strong army of brutes sailing faster than they could comprehend. The Kuyterci army ripped holes in the ground and out came lava, which they threw onto some of the incoming ships and the sea, creating huge spikes of rocks. But it wasn't enough to get rid of the Eldonvillians. Zaula created a tsunami-like wave that nearly sank the ships but these were some mighty war ships that they weren't prepared for. The samurais started to use their fire powers to burn away the rock, which slowly melted from the intense heat. It turned into a grey, rocky slop rather than a barricade to stop the ships. Once again, holes were ripped out into the ground and there was lava coming out of them, thrown onto the decks of the ships. It didn't do much. Some soldiers got ready to use catapults and more machines but the samurais had already reached the coast.

They cried their war cries and sprinted at the Kuyterc soldiers, who were continuously fighting back fiercely. Most of the samurai hadn't even got off the ship. There were just too many samurai for this raid. The soldiers then started to create fiery waves that burnt away the metal on the Samurai Boats, revealing that these were poorly made boats. Leaftor laughed at the workmanship of the boats and started using vines to slash the samurai that got in the way and it was kind of working, except that they also had to deal with siege machines. They were lifted onto the beaches of the Kuyterc Village and they were hammering any walls and rocks that were put together to stop the Eldonvillian Forces. The samurai started using cavalry, which was unexpected. Not even Okoto ordered this. They had one horseman using a blunt spear to puncture the incoming soldiers and an archer at the back with a crossbow that would shoot arrows at any soldier or civilian they saw. It was quite brutal but there was no intention of death to anyone. The samurai kept trying to come at Ekarto but he escaped from their clutches and fought them off with only a sword he found lying on the ground and his hands and feet. The battle kept going on and some scouts were sent to neighbouring villages and tribes to alert them of the raid and ask for more reinforcements and in just a few minutes, when the enemy was getting hold of the Kuyterc Village, some other soldiers from other tribes and villages came with cavalry and people that were dragging catapults shooting fiery boulders onto the samurai ships. Now, the Fire Army was increased to 403 and they were fighting like hell. The battle raged on for two hours.

The samurai were starting to lose as the new soldiers from the neighbouring tribes were some of the most elite soldiers in the world, the Forgoran Warriors. They were a group of skilled soldiers that were realised and created thousands of years ago. They were feared by the world for their expertise in fighting and building war machinery. They were savage warriors that would act inhumane on the battlefield and when they saw the leaders of the village harassed and beaten and robbed by some samurais, hell broke loose in them and they started spinning and slashing, cutting the throats and backs of the samurais. Some samurais had their heads decapitated and thrown into the sea. The samurai were starting to rage and fight more severely. The samurai were not doing too well.

As Ekarto was mindlessly fighting away at the hordes of samurai, one of the leaders of the Kuyterc Village gave Ekarto a sack full of food and other necessities. It was the youngest one, Kartu.

"Escape, flee, run. Ekarto and everyone else, you must leave. It's not safe here."

"NO! I'm staying here to protect you! I can't let you die here or anything happen to you! I need to protect you! Who else will look after me with such good care like my own grandfather?" Ekarto's eyes started to cry and tears rolled down everyone's cheeks. It was a sad departure and it was more hurtful when Ekarto cried and held onto Kartu like his actual grandfather. Kartu was deeply depressed and emotional. He wiped the tears of Ekarto and showed the tears.

"These tears, they are of love and affection. It has been a pleasure to have you here and my heart is almost crushed by this sadness. But don't cry of sadness and fear! We have support! We'll win, Ekarto, don't you worry. I'll never give up my life and see you so hurt, never. We have the spirits. Look, they're descending!" Then, out of nowhere, the sky ripped open, a phenomenon never before seen and spirits flew down with weapons and grim faces, wiping out the samurais fiercely and destroying the ships. Kartu patted Ekarto on the back, wished them all a good journey and told them to go through the Kuyterc Desert.

"Through there, you will pass a straight path directly to the border. There will be villages in between but either you walk past them or explore them, it's up to you. You have to make it to the Vragos border quickly. And again, I'll see you soon. Take care, kids." They waved and cried as they saw the battle rage on but Leaftor calmed everyone down and told them they'd come with news of victory. After a few minutes they were optimistic of the victory and it motivated them to walk the desert of Kuyterc. Border, here they come.

Kuyterc Desert

They strolled in the sandy and rocky desert, sun scorching their skin. April and Mia already had enough sunbathing and were used to the sun, so they walked without difficulty, although sweating a lot. The others didn't find this too easy. They kept groaning and yawning as they walked, but Ekarto pushed forward only to realise this desert was indeed very short.

"GUYS! I don't know why we are waddling over to the borders! We need to get there fast. It's a short desert. Look, I already see a village over there. Come on, guys!" But his little pep talk was short-lived as he started to feel woozy and fell constantly, his legs giving away. His eyelids felt heavy and droopy and he ultimately fainted in the desert. April and Zaula screamed when they saw this and ran to him to come to his aid, only to find he was not breathing. His heart was still beating but he went quite cold. His face turned a bit pale. Ayron and Leaftor carried him to a nearby shack, where there was a cleric inside. That was convenient.

"Hello, how may I help you?" The cleric replied. He was a young man in his late 20s, perhaps. He was also very thin, almost bony. His nose was crooked and his eyebrows were nearly gone. He had sandy hair and red eyes, a smile that seemed like he had done for years. He wasn't even wearing a cleric's tunic. Just some simple clothes and a hat.

"My friend, Ekarto over here, has fainted. He stopped breathing, his face is pale, he's cold but his heart is still beating. WAKE UP YOU WEAK-LOOKING, PEP-TALKING, PRINCE-BEING BUFFALO," Ayron screamed. The cleric laughed and readied a bed for Ekarto, only that it had many splinters and was very hard.

"This increases his chance of waking up. He would be in lots of pain." He then explained he could've been under some spell, perhaps from the samurais but it was hard to tell as there was never a spell like this in his knowledge.

"WELL, DO SOMETHING FOR THE LOVE OF MY PARENTS!" The cleric was giggling again but he was terrified when Hina picked him up by the collar and threw him against the wall, dagger at his neck.

"You better do as I say or your last meal will be my knife, understand? Now, fix him. Do something to help." Hina stared right through the cleric's soul, her voice steady and emotionless. The cleric was dropped onto the floor and he speedily tried some methods on him, which only fixed his pale face.

"This is unusual. No one goes under a spell that some spiritual fire can't break. Spiritual fire breaks all spells. Most, anyway. Why isn't this one working?" This only made everyone more worried. He performed his methods even faster but the fire wasn't working. He sprayed water on Ekarto's face but nothing worked. Then, out of options, he poured some other spell on his body.

"This is a resurrection spell. Now, this doesn't mean he's dead. I just can't tell what's happened. All we can do is wait.

If he doesn't wake up in a few minutes, he's probably dead or under a trance which can't be broken. He'd die if he was in there for too long anyway, so we'll just have to wait. Be patient." Everyone sat down on some benches and kept worrying for Ekarto, who looked peaceful and well-rested in whatever he was under. And, no, it wasn't a spell.

"Where am I?" Ekarto was in a dark room, no floor or walls or sky. It was all black around him and no one was there. Then a bigger version of his face came up in front of him but it was slightly different – older, in one way or another.

"Hello, Ekarto. I'm your father, Okarto." Ekarto couldn't believe it. He was actually speaking to his father, who'd been dead for so long! He bowed in respect but Okarto shook his head.

"I'm your father, not a saint. Calm down. I understand, you've been through a lot and now you get to see me for the first time in your life." They both were ecstatic to see each other, son and father meeting for the first time.

"Why am I here? Why is this place so dark?"

"This place is a reflection of your thoughts and ideas, your moods and feelings."

"So, is this my mind? Because my mind is very dark."

"Yes." Okarto was not wrong. Ever since Ekarto had learnt that his father was killed by Okoto, his mind had been plagued with pessimistic and worrying thoughts that turned him very unbalanced.

"Listen, Ekarto, I haven't got much to say other than I am proud of you. You've done things that not even I could do."

"What?"

"You lived. You see, Okoto was intending to kill you when you returned from Silk Village and he tried through the very handshake you did with him." Ekarto could remember the handshake with Okoto when he first met him.

"How could that have killed me?"

"There was a death spell written on it. It was meant to make you tired and kill you in your sleep but somehow you survived." He could also remember the sudden drowsiness he felt once entering the house. That was supposed to kill him? Wow!

"It's nice to see my very son in front of me. My son, who I thought I was never going to see. I can't express how happy I am. Is it the same for you?" Ekarto also couldn't express it. His father! The very one who turned things well for Silk City! Heck, he created it! Forget Silk City, his actual father! Though it felt weird that his father in Silk Village wasn't his real father.

"Dad, it's nice to have someone to lean on after all this. After I found out who my real family was, I felt devastated as I didn't have anyone to help me. And now, look, you are here." Okarto was pleased just to hear his son's voice. He hugged Ekarto and even tried to play Gargwon with Ekarto. Although Okarto was known to be a master at Gargwon, he lost against Ekarto. Ekarto talked about how Ayron is the ultimate Master at the game.

"It's nice to have friends like him. He's like your brother."

"He is. I wish I had a real sibling." Ekarto looked sad. He really didn't have any siblings or companions to support him when things got tough. Okarto was smiling and was letting him in on a secret.

"Well, you kind of already have a brother. And no, it's not Ayron."

"Who?" Ekarto's face slightly lit up, but he was deeply confused.

"I can't tell you! You'll have to see for yourself." Ekarto was thinking about Leaftor but other than that no one appeared in his mind. Nevertheless, he was happy at least to see Okarto and talk to him. The name Okarto sounded cool and epic to him. And to meet him? A man like that to be his father? He was extremely joyous. He was going to hug Okarto again but he saw a white sheet over his face and could hear people crying. He instantly woke up from his dream, spitting the white cloth away and bouncing off a bed that hurt his back.

"WHO MAKES BEDS LIKE THESE? UGH!" Everyone in the shack, even the cleric, were happy and shocked to see him and hugged and cheered for Ekarto. Ekarto was awake! He was ruffled in his hair by Ayron and they paid the cleric a lot of money. He was happy to have so much money and bowed in respect.

"I'll have enough money to buy my mama some new clothes. She keeps wearing mine."

The little team were walking towards the village they could see far away and because Ekarto was so exhausted, he had to sit down and admire the village to see there was a little festival going on there. Everyone's eyes were stolen by the festival, especially the food and colours.

"Ekarto! Look at this! A festival! Can we go, please?" Mia pleaded with him but he didn't respond. Then he was thrown on the sand by Hina and there was a dagger at his throat.

"You do as I say or else your last meal will be my knife. Understand? Now, let us go to the festival." Ekarto was already exhausted but he couldn't imagine Hina acting like this. Perhaps it was another dream? But it felt so real. So, he let them go and out of nowhere his legs started to feel fine. He was full of energy and he was drawn into the festival too. He ran over to the village where chaos ensued.

The Festival of Tao

Ayron was the first to walk to the Festival, where he was immensely excited about going inside but before he could go in, he noticed there was a guard at the door. He was monitoring everyone that came in and was a big man with muscles that were way too large for someone with legs so small and skinny. He had a weird uniform on and Ayron couldn't tell where he was from. He then saw a sign. It had green circles around the powers of air and fire and allowed anyone who didn't have a power. For Ayron, Ekarto, Mia and Hina, this was an easy one. They could just walk right in, display their powers and could enjoy the festival. Ayron went in first, blasted a dead leaf nearby him and was pushed inside the village. He devoured much of the food he could find. Ekarto went in and created a flame in his hand. Somehow he wasn't recognised, even with his attire. He was pushed inside the village just like Ayron, pulling Ayron away from the food station. Leaftor dressed up as an old traveller from the Kuyterc Desert. He was asked some questions but Leaftor knew better and was let in. Then Mia and Hina were let in as they didn't have any powers. Now it was hard for April and Zaula to get in as they had powers forbidden by the guard, so Zaula asked Hina secretly (through the back wall) to throw her some clothes. She threw some clothes that had many badges and logos stitched and sewn onto it, making her look important and inspiring. She was saluted and welcomed as a 'Veteran Admiral of Tao'. Zaula was happy she was able to get in successfully and cheered when she saw her friends and started dancing and eating, enjoying. Now it was April's turn.

April had nothing to wear or nothing to disguise as. She asked Hina for more clothes but these were for men, and she was a woman. She had no other choice, so she put on her clothes and discarded her royal clothes into a sack she found lying around conveniently. She walked to the entrance, where her hair was tied up in a bun and there was a twig carved to look like a hairpin. She looked confident but the guard stopped her right there. He was looking at April's attire and signalled for her to leave.

"Why can't I come in?"

"You're wearing a disguise. Leave."

"But I am a man!"

"How? Look at you, you're clearly a woman. You've got a woman's face, not a man's one."

"How would you know if my face belongs to a man or woman?"

"Simple. I can tell if the person is a man or woman through their face. Now, leave, please, or I will use force."

"But my friends are in there!"

"Madam, you are not a man. Maybe a madman but not a man. Besides, you have the physique and voice of a woman." This was hard to argue with but April had another plan up her sleeve or sleeves. Surely her friends were there, waiting for her. Yes, she said it already but the guard didn't really hear her.

"My friends are in there!"

"Oh, really? Pick them all out." April tried looking for her friends but they weren't in sight. She was looking and looking but they weren't found.

"I know my friends are in there! I saw them go in! I can't see them now but I will be able to."

"You have to leave, now. If you don't have any powers, you may come in."

"I don't have any." The guard smacked his forehead in disbelief and was laughing.

"You should've said that a long time ago! You don't need to disguise yourself as a man to celebrate this event! Who said only men could go in? You can go in now, I trust you. Though you were a spy or something. You're amusing to me." He pushed April inside the village wall and April tried to find Hina, who was wolfing down some of the desserts in the food stations.

"THANKS FOR EVERYTHING, HINA." Hina was startled when she heard April and almost spat out her food. But she turned around and faced April.

"What did I do? You came in perfectly fine."

"Why did you have to give me a man's clothes? I'm a woman! Anyone can see that!" A woman was walking past April and saw her ridiculous outfit.

"Next time, don't steal clothes from your husband."

"I AM NOT MARRIED." April was extremely furious by now at Hina and then she found the rest of her friends dancing to the music. It was a band of Tao Villagers playing various instruments with Tao Dynasty flags raised in the air. Then she realised something.

This village was a Tao Dynasty Colony.

She ran over to Ekarto, who was starting to eat as he was hungry and told him this village was owned by the Tao Dynasty.

"So what?"

"It means if they find out who you are, they'll kill you! They are some brutal people, I know it." Ekarto also realised what mess he had just put himself in and alerted Ayron, Leaftor, Zaula and Mia. Hina was told by April, so they started thinking of ways to escape.

Now, you might ask why they had to escape.

Because they were considered enemies of the Emperor.

Leaftor, April and Zaula had powers that were considered as forbidden powers to the Emperor.

Hina was a bandit. She was a criminal.

Mia was from Cabourice, a country located next to Eldonville which was sort of taken over by Eldonville. She could be a spy.

Ekarto and Ayron came from Eldonville. They would be enemies of the Dynasty.

Now do you understand?

They quickly devised a plan that, when the festival leader raised the party level to the MAX, they would escape as the guard wouldn't be there anymore because even the guard would be partying, but it was hours until the party would reach that stage, so they had to wait.

The festival was celebrating the birthday of a Tao officer named Khea Tzindo, in case you didn't know. He was the Tao leader of the village and it was on this day he was turning 42 years old. They were very scheduled with his party and surprisingly he was the leader of the festival too. He was singing and dancing on the stage, the crowd cheering for him.

There was a huge pile of presents and gifts on one side of the village walls and the houses were decorated with banners and paintings honouring the Tao Dynasty. Although the villagers were under control of some people they never asked for, they were happy with them. They were willingly celebrating their own rulers that came in and conquered their land! This was the sign that the Tao Dynasty was a popular one and people like its leaders and governing systems. That was the empire Ekarto dreamed of.

There were lots of stations in the festival. Of course, there were lots of food stations but there were also fortune telling ones, costume ones, flag stations, magic tricks, dancing equipment and finally merchandise for the Tao Dynasty, like clothes and collectables. There were high walls around the village, supposedly made from sheets of paper and cotton sewn together and stood up with tall wooden poles. It was to cover the festival and make sure everyone was safe and no thief could escape. It was a festival well-planned, well-made.

The sun was starting to go down and the lights and torches started to light up. In the Tao Calendar, it was the day called 'Choyan', a day where people were not allowed to be outside their homes in the night. This was because on this very day, in Tao Mythology, a female warrior named Zhai Koni was murdered by some 'Disbelievers' when protecting the Tao King. It was in the night when she was killed and it was good to be respectful to her martyrdom and not go out, lest her soul waking up from her rest and causing chaos for not being able to be at ease. It was a weird yet true story and it was a Tao custom to not be out at night to make sure she can rest. It was also believed that on 'Choyan' Zhai was at her angriest. And that was why the festival had to nearly come to an end.

The Tao Officer, Khea, was announcing that it was a pleasure to be alive and well at his age and was announcing the party to go to its MAX for just a few minutes until nightfall when they had to stay in their homes. Then the guard went inside the village and started to enjoy the festival. He ate the food and joined Khea on the stage. It turned out that the guard was Khea's cousin! They had a blast. It wasn't so much of a blast for Ekarto and the rest. They quickly snuck out, leaving their disguised clothes behind near the entrance. Underneath was their real clothes. They dashed around the village and straight up ahead, where there was a long winding path. They walked the path and were exhausted from the festival.

"Whew, that was fun!" Ayron exclaimed. They were all sitting on the floor and panting from all their walking.

"It was quite fun, yes. We have been through a lot," Ekarto said. Then he started to stand in front of his little group and cleared his throat. "I was thinking for a long time that we should have a team name. What do you think?" Everyone nodded and was thinking of a name for them.

"Wonder Stars," Leaftor said, "It was the name of a music band back in my days. Travelled all around the world. Talked about peace." No one really liked the sound of that. Leaftor looked embarrassed.

"Team Ekarto!" Zaula said.

"I was going to say that!" April exclaimed. But no one liked the sound of that either. They agreed it shouldn't have had to be focused on him only.

"What's Okoto's Army name?" Hina asked.

"Okoto's Army? They don't have a name," Ekarto replied.

"Then let's have an army name for us. We will be fighting his army after all." Then Ayron had an idea.

"The Seven." Everyone looked at him, confused.

"That's so bland!"

"Needs more in it."

"I think we could use a bit more drama. Some KAPOW, if you know what I mean."

"I think it's perfect." Then everyone looked at Ekarto, Mia and Leaftor agreeing with him.

"Think about it, we are seven people. Me, Ayron, Leaftor, Zaula, Mia, Hina and April. We don't need anything too fancy. The Seven is a perfect name. Who knows? History will remember us as 'The Seven'." It made a bit more sense but they were still rooting for Team Ekarto or, for Leaftor, the Wonder Stars.

"Well, maybe we could have The Seven Heroes?"

"No."

They got their energy back after randomly talking for a few minutes and The Seven walked continuously until they could see a sign. Border to Vragos or the Central City.

Ayron, the Teacher

They went towards the Vragos Sign and had ended up in another village, whereas this one looked more sophisticated and advanced than anything they'd ever seen. It had tall and massive buildings around the centre of the village with houses and markets circling the towers. Then, as The Seven walked up a hill, they saw a small forest they had to go through. It was weird for a forest to be in such a dry landscape with barely any vegetation or pretty much *anything* except for the villages, rock and desert all around them. They had no other option as the forest was closed off by some walls, so it was clear that they had to go through the forest to reach Vragos. The Seven rushed towards the forest but it wasn't looking that small anymore when they reached it. The trees were looming over their heads but The Seven courageously walked into it, finding many peculiar things like fruits, plants, wildlife and a boy urinating on the forest grounds. The women of the group were disgusted and looked away with Leaftor and Ekarto feeling awkward at what they just saw but Ayron cracked into laughter as he was walking towards the light of the forest. Indeed, the forest wasn't too big. They couldn't even call it a forest, more like a farm where the crops had grown too big.

They walked out and then they could see the village more clearly.

The Seven were walking down a path and could see houses in one neat line and on the other side were other buildings like markets, farms, schools and hospitals and such. There was a public transport system where a horse rider would come every few minutes with a huge box made from wood behind, where passengers would sit in, feeling the breeze as the horse raced by and trotted to their destination. There were tall poles with torches burning to illuminate the streets when it was night and painted paths to divide the people and vehicles. They walked down a red path leading to Vragos, which was only a mile away when they saw a woman running towards Ayron.

"Ah, teacher. You came quite a bit late, am I right?" Ayron was confused and was trying to repel the woman but she dragged him inside a school and inside was a class of around 15 children.

"Children, greet your new teacher for today. Sir, what is your name?" Ayron was bewildered and awestruck at the moment but he decided to go with the flow and replied.

"Ayron, miss."

"Good morning, Ayron Sir," The children simultaneously replied, holding their hands up as if to wave at him. But he thought waving involved the hands to actually move, not to stay there like statues. He let the kids sit down and the strange woman ran away, smiling at the children. Ayron didn't understand how to do this but he taught the kids like how they did back at Silk Village.

"All right, then, kids. What are we learning about today?" One of the kids stood up to speak and Ayron, now acting more responsible and confident, chose that child to speak.

"Sir, we are learning about the Tao Dynasty and its history." This was something Ayron had no clue about, so he made up some characters for today's lesson. The Seven walked into the classroom, watched and analysed by the children.

"Sir, who are they?"

"They are my cast! Yes, my cast! Today, we will be learning about the troll of Tao, Gompha." No one had heard of this but Ayron knew how to make up the story as he went along with it.

"We start off when the Tao Army just started to take over the Fire Tribes. You actually live near a Tao colony, so you should know it by now." The children nodded. It was the same village where the festival took place.

"When the Tao Army took over a lot of the Imperial Fire Tribes, something terrible happened. As they were battling the Central City for power, a troll emerged from the Fire Army. He was the sole protector of the Fire Chief and he was a fierce troll who also had a family that was fighting with him. That's why the Central City nowadays is never taken over. Here, I'll show you an example of what you would've seen. My friend here, Leaftor, is going to be the Tao Army and my other friend, Ekarto, is going to be the Fire Army. Come here, it's up to you to re-enact the scene." They reluctantly went over to Ayron and started fighting very unenthusiastically, groaning and slapping each other. The children found this very amusing and giggled.

"Now, I am the troll. Look at me with my family. Hina and Mia, come here and fight the vicious enemy with me! Hurrah!" They both went over to Ekarto and Ayron and started to slap Leaftor. He was just screaming and getting beatings as the children laughed at him.

"Oh no, now the reinforcements have arrived! Quick, April and Zaula, defend your glorious empire!" Now it just became a brutal war between the two sides. They started to throw chairs and objects around and the children joined the battle, screaming and laughing. The building started to shake and wobble as they fought, but then a child saw the strange woman from before, all angry and dragging another man to the classroom.

"REAL SIR IS HERE! CHILDREN! THAT TEACHER IS A FAKE!" Once Ayron heard this, he pushed The Seven out of the classroom and made them run for a nearby horse carriage that was just about to take off. Ayron called for it and the carriage stopped.

"Where to…"

"VRAGOS BORDER NOW." The horse rider clicked her heels and whipped the horse to make it go as fast as lightning. Ayron looked back at the children and screamed, "I WILL SEE YOU SOON, KIDS." Ayron could see them waving back at him and he was happy to be able to teach the class, but not how he intended…

The horse went faster and faster to the Gates until they reached in a few minutes and were dropped off there, met with some guards that looked grim and angry.

"Stop right there, people." The Seven were searched and checked thoroughly but once they were confirmed to be safe, the Gates weren't opened.

"What's wrong? Why aren't the Gates opening?"

"You have to pay taxes. 500 Fire Sparts. Pay up." Now it was impossible to get into Vragos. How were they supposed to pay money that they didn't have? Ridiculous!

"We don't have that money."

"Bad luck, you're going to have to leave then."

"But we have important business there!"

"Leave or else we will arrest you." This was reminding April of her encounter with that very Tao Guard she had to argue with. She was about to stand up and defend her friends until she heard a voice from beyond the Gates.

"Let them in." It was a soldier, clearly from his uniform and shield with his weapons and helmet. He came from the Arctic Kingdom. He was clearly of a higher rank than those guards as he had four stripes on his sleeve whereas the guards only had two. The soldier was repeating himself again.

"Why should we let them in? They have to pay taxes."

"Do travellers have to pay taxes?"

"No. They won't have local currency."

"Well, clearly these people are travellers. Look at their clothes, none of them are native to the Fire Tribes." It was true. The Seven didn't come from the Imperial Fire Tribes. Technically Ekarto did but that would've caused more problems.

"All right, we'll let you in. If anything happens, report it to the Arctic Army. It's not our responsibility." They started to walk as the Gates slowly opened, and beyond it was nothing new – a rocky, barren landscape except this one was darker and more warped. The Seven were led by the soldier and they walked into Vragos, the Gates closing behind them with a mighty clunk.

Vragos

"Hey, my name is Hikari. Means light. I'm an elite soldier in the Arctic Army, just passed my Elite Soldier Trainee exam a few months ago. Who are you guys?" The Seven were quite reluctant in telling their names but they trusted Hikari.

"My name is Queen April, leader of the Forest Kingdom. That's Leaftor, a veteran from Eldonville. That's Ayron, some villager from the Silk Village in Eldonville. That's Mia, princess of a kingdom in Cabourice, forgot the name. That's Hina, a bandit. That's Zaula, a Gate Guard from Eldonville and finally that's Ekarto, prince of Eldonville." Hikari didn't understand what April just said but he was stunned when he found out who Ekarto was.

"Woah, that's cool. Ekarto, how is Okoto as a father?" Ekarto groaned and then explained that he was the son of Okarto, blah blah blah, you get the story.

"Ah, I see. Okoto is a horrible man. A—"

"A GREEDY, INSOLENT BUM THAT THE DEMONS GAVE TO US AND A STUPID, IDIOTIC, ARROGANT AND UGLY PERSON THAT SMILES TOO MUCH. I WANNA RIP HIS MOUTH OFF HIS FACE AND BEHEA—Okay that was too much from me hehe," Ayron said (not) calmly. Hikari liked Ayron's personality, a feisty and funny guy from Eldonville. He was happy to be with a group of travellers like them. He had never encountered anyone like The Seven.

They were walking and walking (not much happened) until they saw a fort. Ekarto saw a vision at that moment where he saw that the fort was the house of the Stones but there were some guards that made sure no one could reach the stones. Hikari and the rest kept marching away from the path but Ekarto stopped them.

"WAIT!"

"What? I thought we needed to get to the stones?"

"Yes! They're inside that fort!"

"Ah, the Spirits' Demise. It's a great attraction for tourists. Want to check it out?"

"I need to release the spirits in there. That's why I came here in the first place." Hikari looked confused but he just nodded and led The Seven to the fort, where there were some drunk guards there, drinking and dancing.

"WHOOOO! OH, LOOK, I SEE SOME DRAGONS COMING TOWARDS US! YAY, I LOVE VRAGOS!" They were fat, hairy people that had clothes almost ripping out of their trousers. Their hats were strapped tightly around their 'necks', all their skin trapped in the space. Their voices seemed constricted and choked but they were too drunk to realise that. Whilst they seemed to be the worst guard in existence, they couldn't just barge through. Leaftor started thinking of what Okarto did to attract the Tando Ingots many years ago. He asked April for some paint for his face, which she always carried around and Hina for some stolen women's clothes. He made himself look like a woman and ran like a penguin to the drunk guards, his heels kicking his back. The guards were staring at Leaftor.

"Yoo-hoo! Come here, guards!" The guards were intrigued and Leaftor started to sway his hips and step back and taunt the guards, making them more interested.

"That's my wife, there, she is my beautiful wife. Oh, where have you been?"

"No, that's my girlfriend. Did you know she was?"

"No, that's my mother. Ma, I'm coming for you!"

"You can only find out if one of you can catch this rock! The first to return it to me gets me!" Leaftor threw a pebble with all his might, sending it to wherever it went (Legend has it that the pebble is still there). The guards were running towards the direction of the pebble but because they were so drunk, they ran around and passed out, their large bodies slamming themselves against the floor. Leaftor quickly took off the women's clothes and rubbed the paint off his face, Zaula splashing some water onto his face to clean it.

"And that, ladies and gentlemen, is how you get rid of drunk and fat guards." There was a round of applause for him and he gave his clothes back to Hina, who put them back in her sack and strapped it to her back to keep them safe.

They walked inside the fort, where the door was open (The guards seriously weren't doing a good job.) They went through the corridor until they found a backyard with three stones laid in a triangle formation. They had cracks and carves in them, all of them glowing in a different colour. Ekarto grabbed a big stone and with no hesitation, he slammed the rock against the stones but they flashed red, as if he wasn't doing the right thing. He was confused. Shouldn't the stones be opening by now? He kept hammering the other rocks but none of them opened. He slammed himself against the ground and screamed in agony as his arms were aching from each throw. He then saw another vision. It was a vision of Eldon, kneeled down on the floor and speaking to the stones. He was saying chants that would break the stones open and they almost did but then he saw some soldiers shooting him with arrows. He was arrested and taken back to Eldonville. This showed that Ekarto had to recite chants and pray, in spite that the stones would arise and the spirits would be free. He kneeled like Eldon did and chanted and prayed. He didn't feel anything until he felt a weird feeling in his core, his gut. It felt lighter and springier and he saw the stones glowing more, faint voices chanting with him. He recited more and more and felt the temptation to stop as it took a long time. He was encouraged by his friends and Okarto was also heard chanting with him. He kept praying and chanting and he heard screams behind him but he didn't move. He knew it was some chaotic spirit drawing him back. He continued to chant and chant and at last there was an explosion.

The Stones Arise

The fort behind Ekarto eroded away and the whole ground around them turned from dark to light. The explosion came from the stones and when the smoke faded away, Ekarto was in lots of pain but was staring at the Stones. He could see that they were starting to move and they fidgeted and cracked. Then there were three loud pops and the stones were shot into the sky, spiritual energy filling the space. Then, the most wonderful thing happened. Three spirits curled up and in pain, sprung up and laughed and cheered. They were in so much joy, it was hard to express. Then they looked at Ekarto and relieved him of his pain. He brought his friends up as they had been knocked out from the explosion and Ekarto was glowing with his friends. The spirits descended and were smiling.

"Hello, Ekarto. I am very thankful for what you have done. I have been trapped in there for 10,000 years, oh, it was such a long time. Thank you, Ekarto. The debt I can never give back to you is enormous." The spirit hugged Ekarto and introduced itself.

"My name is Miwi. I was sending these visions to you. The blue spirit next to me is Harki, spirit of strength and wisdom. The green spirit next to me is Fenoi, spirit of luck and wealth. I am the spirit of good and evil, meaning that I decide what is good and evil in the spirit realm. I was told that I would be released by you and I would give you a reward." He twirled in happiness and gave a box to Ekarto.

"Inside is 100,000 Lon Pieces, Moon Clan currency. Meet with the Moon king and create an alliance with him. Keep using this money as it is accepted by everyone in the world, even Eldonville. If you can use this wisely, you'll create a strong army. I am also going to give you all good luck from Fenoi and strength from Harki. These only work when you truly need them. I will be protecting you from evil but only that which I can protect you from. I will also guide you along the way to fight Okoto. Ever since that day he became King, the world has been in constant agony and unbalance. I will help you all to make sure Eldonville becomes a righteous kingdom again. Anything else that you want?" Ayron exclaimed for a plate of food and Hikari asked for a promotion. Hina asked for more money and Leaftor asked to be able to meet Okarto again. Ekarto only asked for his fate to carry out as it was supposed to be.

"All of these will be fulfilled and those who want things that haven't been said, don't worry. The silent wishes will always be fulfilled. We're spirits of the highest order. We'll give you what you want as long as you do noble deeds."

"Wait, why were you guys trapped in there for so long?" Ekarto asked.

"We were punished for apparently acting evil and trying to plot the fall of all spirits. We were imprisoned but it was supposed to be for a few days as they found out we weren't plotting anything. Unfortunately, they couldn't lift the stones as it was in human power to lift it up. Eldon was the only person besides you to try but he failed and you succeeded. I will make sure the world knows about you. In case you were wondering why we still look so young, it's because the stone preserves age for us. It's quite confusing but anyhow. I look fabulous." The two other spirits agreed. Harki lit up and floated in front of Ekarto.

"I'm saying my last biggest thanks. What you have done for us is a deed with innumerable benefits. Your journey to become the new king of Eldonville will not be easy, but we will try our best as allowed by the highest spirits to make your missions as easy as we can. We will always be with you in return for releasing us after thousands of years. Goodbye!"

Ekarto felt happy but unaccomplished. He wanted to do more.

"Don't worry, Ekarto. This is just the beginning. In the end, once Okoto is finished, you will be greatly accomplished and powerful. Remember in life that you must climb each rung of the ladder as it was made. You may fall if you skip too many rungs. Apply this logic to your life, and you will feel good about yourself. My dad told me this during my training to be a spiritual councillor," Miwi said, reading his mind. Ekarto was astonished that the spirits could read his mind, and was reassured that he could do the tasks he had to do in the future, no matter how large or small.

The spirits started to ascend but then Miwi returned in a flash.

"Oh! I almost forgot. I have to teleport you to the Moon Clan. Just wait, it'll be in no time."

"WAIT! MY FOOD."

A sudden bright flash appeared in front of them. Within a fraction of a second, the light disappeared. They ended up in the Moon Clan, all well and fine. They were in front of a house and it was apparently made for The Seven. Hikari wasn't with them anymore but The Seven would always remember him, the elite soldier that helped them along the way to the fort. Ayron's food and Hina's money was still there and they were excited to see the immense mansion in front of them. They walked into the mansion, impressed by the vast rooms and halls inside. There was a strong smell of sandalwood and lotus oils in the house, and the floors and stairs were painted in blue and grey, standing out from the rather boring wooden interior. Everyone went to their rooms and rested. A lot had happened in a few days, and they were exhausted. Ekarto lied in his bed and thought about what had just happened from the day of his dream and what could happen in the future. The future was quite daunting, but he felt confident and was willing to do anything to avenge his father. The world wanted a stop to Okoto's Empire. Ekarto, on the other hand, was only determined to slay Okoto for the death of his father and torment Okoto.

Okoto was ready to bring down Harro, and the rest of the world with Ekarto. Nothing would stop him.

Not even the spirits, or Ekarto.